It was an uncanny sensation. More than a momentary attraction. What it might become, he didn't know.

He spotted her immediately, standing by the Christmas tree. The lights sent sparkles glinting through her hair. When she saw him, her eyes lit up, too, and she smiled almost as if she had been waiting for him.

Suddenly there seemed to be no one else in the crowded house, no one at the party, just the two of them.

"Hello, Mark. I'm glad you came," Coryn greeted him.

All around, the party sounds swirled while they talked of many things. Yet Mark had the feeling that there was so much more they had to talk about. He felt that they were on the brink of something happening between them. Something serious. Important.

JANE PEART

Award-winning and bestselling author Jane Peart grew up in North Carolina and was educated in New England. Jane and her husband now reside in Northern California, which is often a setting for her novels.

In more than twenty books and her bestselling Orphan Train West series, Jane has brought to readers the timeless themes of family, faith and committed love.

THE RISK OF LOVING

JANE PEART

Published by Steeple Hill Books™

STEEPLE HILL BOOKS

Steeple
Hill™

ISBN 0-373-87003-5

THE RISK OF LOVING

"Weeping may endure for a night, but joy cometh in the morning."

—*Psalms* 30:5

November

Chapter One

On a rain-swept night the weekend before Thanksgiving, holiday travelers thronged San Francisco International Airport.

In the passenger lounge of Westair's northbound Flight 84 Mark Emery glanced over the top of his *Newsweek* as a slender brunette came through the security check enclosure. She wore a belted raincoat and high-heeled boots. Her dark, shoulder-length hair glistened with raindrops. She stood for a minute looking around for an empty seat.

Mark watched as she made her way across the crowded waiting room. She had a confident, graceful walk. Stepping over assorted baggage cluttering the aisles, she took a seat opposite his. There was something familiar about her but he couldn't place her. Could he have seen her at some local function he'd covered for the *Daily Sentinel*? He'd been to dozens of them. Community and political affairs were newsworthy events in the small northern California town of Rockport. Still, he couldn't recall where or when they might have met. He returned to the article on the Middle East.

Coryn Dodge stared blankly through the plate-glass window out to the landing field. Planes taxied into position, lights glowing on the rain-slick tarmac. Carts piled with luggage swerved and snaked toward yawning cargo bins. Planes took off. Planes going different places carrying people to happy homecomings.

Coryn knew she should feel happy, too, and be looking forward to spending Thanksgiving with her parents. She felt guilty that she didn't.

If her father hadn't phoned, she might have waited to see if Jason called from Detroit. But there had been something in her father's voice, an uncharacteristic tension in his tone. When he reminded her she had not been home since last spring, a sliver of guilt had pricked Coryn, and she'd quickly agreed to come for Thanksgiving.

She'd been lucky to get a reservation at this time of year. There was only one available seat on the flight to San Francisco. In order to make the connecting flight to Rockport she'd had to leave L.A. right away. Before she left for the airport she'd called Jason but only got his message machine. She hated leaving with so many unresolved questions about their relationship. But what relationship? Jason had never made any commitment. They'd never discussed a future together. The enduring love Coryn had always secretly hoped to find was probably a dream. Not a nineties kind of thing.

Impatient with herself, Coryn dug into her tote bag and pulled out the magazine she'd bought at the airport newsstand. She slipped on her glasses and started flipping through the pages, hoping to find an article to distract her.

Mark Emery stirred restlessly in the vinyl chair and glanced at his watch. The flight to Rockport took an hour and forty-five minutes. He'd get home around ten. Home. Alone.

Mark felt the old bitterness twist within, as it always did when he thought about it. It wasn't fair. But whoever said life was fair?

He looked around the waiting room at the various groups of happy people bound for family gatherings. Even crowded airports were strangely lonely places. It didn't really matter where he was. He could spend Thanksgiving in the airport for all he cared.

At that moment the young woman seated across from him lifted her head from the magazine she was reading. Their gazes met. Even with her glasses on she was amazingly attractive. The lenses magnified the size and color of her intensely blue eyes.

Their look held for a minute. Coryn wondered where she had seen the man across the aisle before. He was good-looking in a tweedy sort of way. His thick brown hair was salted with some gray at the temples. His features were good, his eyes thoughtful, his expression held both intelligence and humor. His destination must be Rockport. She searched her memory. Could she possibly have met him somewhere when she was home last spring?

Just then the PA system crackled to life: "Attention, all passengers ticketed for Westair Airlines Flight 84 to Rockport. We are overbooked for this flight. If two passengers will volunteer to give up their seats they will be placed on the next available flight and receive a voucher for a free trip anywhere on our route."

An uncomfortable silence spread throughout the waiting room. People stirred in their seats. The low murmur of voices followed. Still, no one got up and moved to the ticket counter. Most of the assembled passengers were on their way home from college or business trips, eagerly awaiting the flight home to be with family and friends. Nobody wanted to give up their seat.

Coryn was aware of the uneasy pall that fell on the holiday mood in the room after the announcement. A few hours' difference in *her* arrival time would not matter that much, she reflected. Her parents had a social engagement anyway and would be gone all evening. Why not give up her seat on this flight and take the next one?

Mark folded his *Newsweek,* stuffed it into the pocket of his duffel bag, got up and ambled over to the ticket counter. He was certainly in no hurry to get home. Without Ginny the weekend loomed dismal. He'd given Mrs. Aguilar, the housekeeper, the holiday weekend off. Why not give up his seat?

At the ticket counter, Mark was rewarded with a big smile of relief from the harried-looking agent behind the desk. He waited while his ticket was rewritten and his travel voucher made out. Mark became aware of movement beside him. He turned. The young woman who'd been sitting near him now stood beside him.

"I guess we're the altruistic ones in the bunch. Or maybe just the only ones with no holiday plans." Immediately he realized the remark he had meant jokingly did not amuse her.

She inclined her head slightly, forced a smile. He was grateful for the ticket agent's interruption, "Here you are, Mr. Emery, and many thanks."

Mark pocketed his ticket and voucher. As he walked back to his seat, he heard the agent say, "Good evening, Miss Dodge."

Dodge? That was the name of the Rockport man rumored to be challenging the incumbent for an assembly seat in the next election. Neil Dodge, a successful contractor and civic leader. Was that his wife? No, too young. Besides, the agent had called her *Miss* Dodge. Maybe she wasn't related to Neil Dodge at all. Still, he may have seen her before at some fund-raising event or other.

He felt a little sheepish for the remark he had made to her. He was not good at small talk or socializing. Out of practice. Even among his colleagues at the newspaper he had a reputation for being a loner. A curmudgeon? Shari had been the one who was outgoing, friendly, vivacious. Everyone loved Shari. She made friends easily. Since she was gone, everything had changed.

Flight 84 was called and passengers gathered up packages, bundles, belongings and trooped out through the gate to board the plane. Mark watched them go, grimly wishing he hadn't been so impulsive. The next flight north wasn't due for at least two hours. He looked around uneasily. Suddenly, the waiting room, filled with people and voices a few minutes before, was quiet and empty. Except for two. Himself and Miss Dodge. He glanced over at her, seated on the opposite side of the room, apparently preoccupied with her own thoughts.

Mark stood up. He'd read his magazine cover to cover. He thought he'd better get something else to read until the next flight north arrived. He strolled out to the corridor, passed people worriedly studying posted arrival and departure bulletins. Weather seemed to be affecting all eastbound flights originating in San Francisco, as well as those due. A long list of "delayed" or "canceled" notices followed destination names and numbered flights. It might be a long night.

Mark checked out the newsstand but nothing appealed to him so he strolled the labyrinthine halls of the airport, leisurely browsing the gift-shop windows. Something for Ginny for Christmas? No. Too early. Anyway, he wasn't sure what she'd like this year.

At the entrance of one of the airport restaurants, Mark stopped to examine the menu on the door. Knowing the best he could expect on the flight was a soft drink and small bag of peanuts, he decided he might as well eat. There was a line, made up, he guessed, of stranded passengers. He took a place at the end of it. Overheard snatches of conversations relayed the usual horror stories of delayed plans and canceled flights. He listened with sympathetic amusement. A few minutes later someone stepped in behind him. When he turned his head, he saw it was her, his fellow passenger from Flight 84.

Remembering her lack of response to his first attempt at conversation, he hesitated. Yet, he couldn't ignore her. He nodded and said, "Hi."

This time she smiled—an astonishingly lovely smile. "When in doubt, eat, right?"

He grinned. "Well, I've taken the flight to Rockport before and I can guarantee you that we won't get fed on the plane. And who knows how long we'll be delayed here. Might as well take advantage of being in San Francisco."

"At least they'll probably have sourdough French bread."

The line moved slowly ahead of them. A hostess escorted people to the few vacated tables. Obviously other passengers were using their waiting time by lingering over dinner and coffee.

"I'm Mark Emery. I'm a reporter on the *Rockport Times.*"

"I'm Coryn Dodge. I've seen your byline. My mother sends me the hometown paper."

"You live in San Francisco?"

"In L.A. At least, I work in L.A."

"Are you on your way home?"

"Yes, I'm spending Thanksgiving with my parents."

They were now at the head of the line. The hostess threaded her way through the tables, approaching them. "Table for two?" she asked, and not waiting to be corrected, "This way, please."

Mark glanced at Coryn and back at the hostess. "Well, we're not—together."

The hostess's arched eyebrows lifted, her forehead puckered. Pursing her lips, she looked around the restaurant with an annoyed expression. "Well…it might be a long wait…" Turning back to them, she asked, "Would you mind sharing a table?"

Mark looked at Coryn, "Would you?"

With only the slightest hesitation, she answered, "No, not at all."

Her problem solved, the hostess smiled. "Good. Please come this way." She moved swiftly over to a corner table a busboy had just cleared.

They sat down and a waiter handed them menus and went away. For a few minutes they studied the selections.

"See anything you like?" Mark asked.

"I'm not really all that hungry. I just thought it would take up some time… Oh, a Cobb salad, I guess."

"I think I'll try the scallops." Mark said. The waiter came back and Mark ordered for them both. "Coffee first?" he asked Coryn. When she nodded, the waiter poured them each a cup then left again.

As she sipped her coffee, Coryn took a good look at the man across the table. He had an intelligent, pleasant expression and might have been downright handsome had it not been that his nose was the slightest bit crooked. However, instead of detracting from his looks, Coryn thought the slight flaw lent a certain ruggedness to his features that she found quite attractive. Suddenly she realized that he was also regarding her thoughtfully. All at once, she felt a little self-conscious. Here they were, two complete strangers, now what?

Mark did not want to force conversation. Yet it seemed worse not to say anything. Besides, he felt obligated. He had been the one to suggest they share a table. He could always employ his reportorial skills. His comfort zone. He cleared his throat.

"Do you like L.A.?"

"Like it?" Her eyes widened as if she was caught off guard by the question. "Actually, I hadn't intended to stay there. The summer after I graduated I went to visit a girlfriend, someone I knew from college. It just sort of happened...I got a job and..."

What had *really* happened was she had met Jason Kramer. They had met at a party, a housewarming for one of Sheila's friends who had just moved into a new condo in Santa Monica. Someone introduced them. One thing had led to another. It was as simple as that. And as complicated.

"What do you do in L.A.?" Mark continued, feeling he was on safe ground. He *was* curious. She had a certain style, a class-act look.

"I work for a public relations firm."

"That sounds interesting."

"Interesting?" She paused as if not quite knowing how to answer him. "That's what I thought, at first. At least my job isn't. We're assigned to certain accounts. What it actually amounts to is a clipping service."

"I gather you're not planning to make a career of it?"

"Hardly."

"What would you rather be doing?"

She looked at him steadily for a full minute as if she didn't quite understand the question.

"I meant," he explained, "if you aren't that sold on your job, there must be some other interest you'd like to pursue. Unless something else is keeping you in L.A.?"

To her relief the waiter reappeared with their order. She had no intention of telling him what kept her in L.A. Or that she might be on the brink of making a change. In her job and her life-style. But you don't pour out your heart to a perfect stranger. At least, she'd never been the type to do so. Besides, she wasn't sure just what she was going to do about anything.

After the waiter left, she asked Mark, "What about you? Were you always interested in newspaper work?"

"Yes. I worked on the school paper in high school, worked as a stringer and in the summer at a local paper. In college, I took a double major in journalism and economics. When I graduated, I got the first job I interviewed for, and that was that. For a year." He smiled. "Ironically, one of the good or bad aspects of being a newspaperman is the urge to move on to another town, a bigger paper."

"How did you happen to come to Rockport?" Coryn found herself curious to know. There was a certain sophistication about Mark that hardly seemed small-town. "The *Times* isn't exactly a metropolitan newspaper."

"Rockport seemed a good place to bring up children."

"You have children?" Coryn felt surprised. It had not occurred to her that Mark Emery was married or a father.

"A little girl. Ginny. Six."

"Does your wife like Rockport?"

His expression changed. He took a sip of coffee. "My wife's dead."

"Oh, I'm sorry, I—"

"Don't apologize. You couldn't have known. It was three years ago. A skiing accident." He paused. "Being a single parent, you have to weigh everything. The job itself isn't the priority. Where it's located is sometimes more important. Now I consider things I might not otherwise, take fewer risks."

Coryn could think of nothing to say to that. Marriage, children, death, all things she had not experienced. She picked up her fork and began to eat.

In a few minutes, Mark commented thoughtfully, "Strange, isn't it? You moved from the north coast to L.A. and I moved from southern California to Rockport."

"The heart has its reasons, as someone said."

Her remark begged exploring. His reporter's instinct prompted, but this time Mark decided against acting upon it. There was a remoteness about her that discouraged intimacy. He studied the young woman sitting opposite him. She had slipped the raincoat off her shoulders and underneath she wore a royal blue cowl-necked sweater that deepened the color of her eyes. Her dark hair waved softly back from ears where small gold hoops swung.

The waiter appeared, refilled their coffee cups. When he left, Mark brought the conversation back to himself.

"Well, *my* reason to move to an area like Rockport was practical. Ginny started first grade this year. I wanted her to grow up in a small community, go to school with the same kids through her school life, kids whose parents I'd know. I wanted to know her teachers, have neighbors who cared about her... In the city, I didn't even know my neighbors' names."

"There's some value in anonymity. In a town like Rockport, there are no secrets. In L.A., nobody knows what you do or cares."

He raised his eyebrows. "And you like that?"

"We're coming from opposite perspectives, as you pointed out. I grew up in Rockport."

"And don't you think small towns have advantages?"

"Sure. But they also have their downside. A town like Rockport doesn't prepare you for another kind of life. It's a real reality shift to move to a big city." Coryn thought of her own naiveté when she'd arrived in L.A. Her expectations had ended in disillusionment. But that wasn't something she wanted to talk about, either. Mark was looking at her intently as if waiting for her to go on.

Suddenly Coryn thought, *I'm talking too much.* That was the danger with as good a listener as Mark Emery. Talking to a stranger was easier than to a friend. Safer. Chances were they'd never see each other again after tonight.

The waiter returned to see if they wanted dessert. They refused, but asked for coffee refills. Coryn had indicated separate checks when their order was taken, so when they finished their coffee and got up to leave, there was no discussion about who paid what. They both used credit cards and made their way out of the restaurant.

Coryn told Mark she wanted to make a phone call and added that she'd see him back in the waiting room.

"See you later," he replied. "And thanks for the company at dinner," he added.

Coryn smiled as they parted. He was merely being polite, she told herself. But it was nice of him to say, nonetheless.

In the phone booth, she dialed her L.A. number. She wanted to see if Jason had left any message on her answering machine since her last check. There was none.

Coryn sat there for a full minute, got her phone card out of her wallet and dialed Jason's number. It rang and rang, then his taped message came on. "Jason Kramer. Leave a message. If it seems important, I'll get back to you. Cheers."

As she listened for the message to finish, a mixture of emotions swept over Coryn. Recorded, Jason's self-confident manner came off as arrogant. Hadn't her roommate, Sheila, often complained that Jason's tendency for put-downs was offensive? She had defended him, saying, "Oh, he's only kidding." But maybe Sheila was right. She didn't leave a message. She knew he wasn't home, but he sometimes left a personal message for her on his greeting. Coryn replaced the receiver and sat there for another moment. Well, he hadn't left a message for her. It had happened before. Later, he'd offhandedly apologize. But that was Jason. Take it or leave it. Coryn opened the folding doors of the phone booth to take a deep breath just in time to hear the PA announce her flight.

She hurried toward the waiting room. Mark was standing at the entrance. He motioned her forward. He held open the door to the field for her and together they went down the steps out to where the plane was loading.

The wind was fierce as they walked across the wet tarmac to board. Coryn hurried up the small metal steps and into the plane. She immediately noticed that the plane was nearly full with passengers who had boarded in Sacramento. At the door, the flight attendant, taking them for a couple, said, "Sorry, there are no two seats together, just singles."

Coryn moved down the aisle to an empty seat. She stowed her luggage in the overhead compartment then got settled, safety belt fastened, as the plane taxied down the runway for takeoff. Finally, they were airborne. Without wanting to, her thoughts returned to Jason. For months he'd occupied so much of her life. She was beginning to realize their whole relationship might have been a waste of time. It would be a relief to be away from L.A. for a while.

Mark pushed the lever at the side of his seat to move it into a reclining position. At last he was on his way home. Home? Without Ginny.

He'd left Ginny in San Rafael to spend the holidays with Shari's parents. They'd always spent Thanksgiving with the Bartons. This year he'd used work as his excuse not to stay over. They accepted that. He wasn't sure they believed it, but he knew they understood. In three years he'd made a lot of progress, but there were still too many memories of other Thanksgivings spent there when Shari was alive.

She'd been their pride and joy, the light of their lives. All those clichés people use to describe the feelings of doting parents of an only daughter fit the Bartons. Since her death, their house had become a kind of shrine to her memory with photos of her everywhere. Shari in her cheerleader outfit, as homecoming queen in high school, at her senior prom and as a bride. Shari had done it all. The only thing she hadn't been able to do was have a baby.

They had adopted Ginny. Then their happiness was complete. For a while at least. He felt a deep, familiar sadness well up in him. It was so unfair. But it had been three years ago. He should be getting over it, shouldn't he?

At Rockport Airport the terminal clock read 2:20 a.m. Too late certainly to call home. Coryn walked outside into the foggy night in hopes of finding a cab or maybe one of the hotel-shuttle vans. Neither was in sight. She'd have to go back inside, phone for a cab. Just then, Mark Emery emerged through the glass doors, carrying his overnight bag and briefcase.

"No one to meet you?"

"I didn't really expect anyone this late."

"I left my car parked here Friday. I'd be glad to drive you home."

Coryn hesitated. "You're sure? It might be out of your way. My parents live in Chestnut Hills, that's quite a way on the other side of town."

"No problem. We live in Kensington Park." He looked at her carry-on and overarm leather tote. "Is that all you have?"

"Yes, I'm only staying through Thanksgiving," she explained as they started walking toward the parking lot.

The night air was damp and smelled of fog. He unlocked his car, a station wagon, and held the door open for her to get into the passenger seat. He went around, got in the other side, turned on the ignition. They pulled out into the curved road leading from the airport.

Fog drifted in eerie yellow swirls in the headlights as they merged onto the freeway. "Looks as though it just opened up enough so we could land, now it's closed down again," Mark said.

"Typical north-coast November," Coryn replied.

"I'm getting used to it. In fact, I like it. The rain, the fog. There's a kind of feeling of being sheltered, protected from the outside world."

"Some call it the Redwood curtain." Coryn glanced at him. "You don't feel confined? I mean, after working in the city I would think you might find living up here too insulated."

"No, not at all. It's better for Ginny. And it's what Shari wanted...what we planned to do if she had lived."

Coryn murmured something she hoped sounded sympathetic.

"It's working out just fine. Great, in fact," he said firmly. He sounded as if he was convincing himself.

They drove the rest of the way mostly in silence, each locked into private thoughts. Mark took the turnoff to Chestnut Hills, one of Rockport's prestigious residential areas. They wound up the twisting tree-lined road.

"Next right, number 183." Coryn directed and Mark swerved into a gravel driveway and pulled to a stop in front of a rambling stucco and timbered house. An old-fashioned lamppost lit the way to an arched stone entrance.

Coryn slung the strap of her tote over her shoulder and opened the car door. "Don't bother to get out. I can manage. Thanks for the ride."

"My pleasure," Mark said. "Good night and have a nice visit with your folks." He watched her until she had opened the door, turned back and waved and gone inside.

The minute Mark turned the key in the lock of his front door he was hit by the emptiness. He quickly switched on the light in the hall, set his suitcase down and stood there for a minute. It still happened, that wave of depression crashing down on him, knowing there was no one to welcome him.

He looked through the mail Mrs. Aguilar had left neatly stacked on the hall table. Nothing important. Mark felt tired but not sleepy.

He went into the kitchen, turned on the light, went to the refrigerator. Ginny's last drawing brought home from school adorned the front of it. A smiling Pilgrim family, complete with a huge orange cat. A Thanksgiving art project, or was this her way of persisting in her plea for a pet? "Just a little kitten, Daddy, please. I'll take care of it, I promise!" Mark smiled. Even at six Ginny knew how to get to him.

Shari would have let her have a kitten. That's for sure. The sharp sensation of loneliness came again. The realization of not having things like this to share with someone. Sometimes the pain was sharp and sudden. Other times just a dull ache.

Somehow, he and Ginny had managed to survive. They had a housekeeper, the efficient Mrs. Aguilar, who adored Ginny, cooked good meals and kept the house, saw that their clothes were washed and ironed. The first year had been the hardest. Now going on three since Shari's accident, they'd managed. Just.

Maybe it was wandering around the San Francisco airport waiting for the next flight north that had put him in this strange mood. The unexpected meeting with Neil Dodge's daughter. He had seen the quick brightening of her eyes in sympathy when he'd told her about Shari. It was as if she'd wanted to say something comforting but was too shy. Sensing that in her had sharpened his own need to share his heart

with someone again. Someone who would understand. It might be crazy. He might be way off base,
but he had sensed a vulnerability in Coryn Dodge
under her poised surface.

He'd like a chance to get to know her better...but
that took time and effort. He'd tried going out after
the first year. Friends had fixed him up with someone
they "knew" he'd like. But nothing had ever worked
out. He knew there was a void in his life, but relationships took time and effort.

Coryn Dodge might be someone he could be interested in. She had been easy to talk to, had listened
with warm empathy...as if she understood.

Mark opened the refrigerator, got out a quart of
milk, poured himself a glass. Coryn Dodge. There
had been something about her, something elusive
that lingered in his mind. Like the scent of her perfume had lingered in the heated car after she got out.

He drained the glass, rinsed it and left it on the
drainboard. That kind of thinking was going nowhere. Theirs had been one of those chance meetings. After Thanksgiving she'd be back in L.A. His
life here would go on. He had a long weekend to get
through somehow, alone.

Coryn let herself in the house. The lamp on the
hall table shed a rosy glow, touching the gold frame
of the mirror on the wall above and gilding the
bronze chrysanthemums in the vase beside it. A note
was propped against the base of the lamp:

Welcome home, darling! We called the airport and were told your connecting flight had

been delayed in Sacramento. Hope it wasn't too awful. There's an apple pie on the kitchen counter. We'll see you in the morning.

Love,
Mother and Dad

Coryn removed her coat, flung it on one of the Queen Anne chairs that flanked the table. She dropped her bag and set down her carry-on, took off her boots and walked stocking-footed down the hall to the kitchen. She heard a low whimpering and the sound of scratching from behind the closed utility-room door. Smiling, she opened it. Ranger, their fourteen-year-old black Lab, came out sniffing and whining deep in his throat.

"Hello, old fella. How are you?" she whispered, bending over to rub his head, scratch his ears. His thick tail swung like a heavy whip as he circled her. He moved stiffly. Coryn realized Ranger was getting older. His arthritis was worse, there was gray around his muzzle. "Good boy." She nestled his head against her shoulder and hugged him. "I know, it's been a long time. I'm glad to see you, too."

Her throat constricted suddenly. She hadn't realized. Away from home, in her mind, everything remained the same. The picture held constant, secure, reassuring. But Ranger was visibly changed. What other changes would she find here?

Chapter Two

Coryn opened her eyes and looked around the bedroom. It had been redecorated for her sixteenth birthday. The furniture was the ivory French Provincial she had requested. Wallpaper, curtains, pillows on the curved window seat were all in her favorite color, blue.

The room had suited her perfectly when she was a teenager. But even when she came home from college on spring break or summer vacations, it had seemed juvenile, though she had not spent much time in it. There was always too much to do. Friends to see, places to go. It had just been a place to sleep or change clothes, to come to and leave from.

Everything in the bedroom was familiar. As if she'd never been away. Yet everything *had* changed. *She* most of all. From sixteen to twenty-six.

Faintly she heard muted sounds, movement, voices from downstairs. Her parents were probably already up, knew she was home.

She got out of bed and looked out the window. Fog dripped from the Douglas firs surrounding the house. She thought of the days of endless smog-hazy sunshine in L.A. and shivered. She was back in "God's country," as natives of the area called it.

In the adjoining pink-tiled bathroom, she splashed water on her face, scrubbed her teeth, brushed and tied her hair back with a ribbon she found in the vanity drawer.

At the doorway of the kitchen, Coryn hesitated a moment, taking in the scene. Cheerful yellow walls, daisy-print café curtains accented the oak cabinets. Pots of red geraniums on the windowsill brightened the gray day outside. Her father stood at the counter, holding the morning paper, scanning the headlines. Her mother sat in the curved breakfast nook sipping a cup of coffee. Coryn realized anew what an extraordinarily good-looking couple her parents were.

Neil Dodge, six-foot and broad-shouldered with iron-gray hair that was perhaps receding a bit these days, was still a handsome man at fifty-five. He had strong features. A prominent nose and high cheekbones in a face tanned from weekends on the golf course or on fishing trips.

Her mother was...well, the only way you could describe Clare Dodge was beautiful, even at this hour of the morning, without makeup. Her silver-blond hair fell in natural waves around her slim shoulders.

"Good morning!" Coryn said as she stepped into the room.

"Darling!" Her mother greeted her happily and got up to hug her. "It's so good to have you home."

Coryn returned the hug and over her mother's shoulder, smiled at her father saying, "Hi, Dad."

"Good to have you home, honey. How was the trip?"

"Not bad at all. Just late." She went over to kiss him. Ranger struggled to his feet from where he had been sprawled on the floor looking up at her hopefully and Coryn bent over and rubbed his ears affectionately. "The flight was overbooked and I had to take the later one."

"I'm not surprised. This time of year," her father said. "I've cooled my heels at San Francisco International myself plenty of times waiting for the fog to lift. It's to be expected coming up the coast. I thought you might have to stay overnight at one of the airport hotels."

"Did you see anyone you know from Rockport in the airport or on the plane?" her mother asked. "Your father usually runs into someone."

"Not exactly. No one I knew. But I did get to have some company in the waiting room. Someone named Mark Emery. He's a reporter for the *Times*. We had dinner together while waiting for our flight. He drove me home."

"Mark Emery, the columnist?" Her father looked interested. "He writes fine, incisive articles. Pulls no punches."

"Sit down and have some breakfast, darling," her mother urged. "What would you like? Waffles? Muffins? Bacon and eggs."

"Just coffee for now. Thanks, Mom."

"That's no breakfast for a growing girl," her father teased. It was a family joke. He'd made the same comment for years at breakfast. "Better eat something. You're too thin."

"Didn't someone say you can't be too thin or too rich?" Coryn slid into the built-in cushioned seat of the breakfast nook.

"I don't know about the too thin but maybe I agree about the too rich." Her father pretended to scowl.

Her mother set down a cup of coffee in front of Coryn. "There's so much to talk about. You never write and when you phone, well, you always seem in a hurry. Tell us all about everything."

"That's a tall order. Can it wait until I get my daily dose of caffeine?" Coryn smiled. Taking a sip, she regarded her mother affectionately, noticing that she seemed a little pale. Still, no one would ever guess her to be fifty-three.

Her mother sat down opposite her and reached over to pat her arm. "I'm so glad you're here. There is so much I want us to do. We'll have to go Christmas shopping, of course, and I'd like to do something special for you while you're here. Wouldn't you like to have a little get-together with some of your old friends? Lora and Cindy both want to see you and—"

"Mom, I'm going to be here only a few days. There won't be much time."

"Clare," her father's voice cut into the conversation. "Are you planning to cook something? All the burners on the stove are on *high*."

"Are they?" Sounding startled, her mother

jumped up. "Oh, dear, I didn't realize—" She
looked flustered and went over to the stove, snapped
the buttons off. Her face was flushed, she darted a
quick anxious look at her husband. "I'm sorry—"

"It's okay, dear. You probably were just excited
at Coryn's being here." Although her father spoke
quietly, obviously checking his irritation, his words
had seemed like a reprimand. "Just be careful, won't
you? The other night when I couldn't sleep, I came
down to make some cocoa and I found the burners
had been left on."

"Oh, my, I didn't know. How could I have done
that?"

Coryn's father put his arm around her mother's
shoulders. "It's okay, dear, it won't happen again,
I'm sure, with Coryn here to check up on you." His
attempt at humor didn't quite come off.

Coryn put her cup down slowly. *What was going
on here?* There was a disturbing friction between her
parents. A definite undercurrent.

"Well, ladies, I better be on my way." Neil
reached for his raincoat, which was hanging on the
peg by the back door that led into the garage. "I
have some bids to go over. You two have a good
day catching up. See you later."

"What time will you be home for dinner, Neil?"

He halted, as if considering. "What say we go out
to dinner tonight? Celebrate Coryn's homecoming?
That way you won't have to worry about shopping
or cooking."

Coryn saw her mother's smile fade. Clare was a
gourmet cook. At other times Coryn had come home

she had taken delight in preparing a special dinner with all her daughter's favorite dishes. It was almost a tradition. Had her father forgotten that? Or was there some hidden meaning in her father's words?

"Of course, dear," Clare replied. "That will be fine."

Neil left, and her mother came back to the table, a bewildered frown creasing her smooth forehead. It was quickly replaced by a bright smile as she said, "That will be fun, the three of us going out. Won't it? Remember we used to do that Friday nights when you were little. Meet Daddy downtown for dinner? An adventure." She glanced at Coryn fondly. "We've missed you so much."

An anxiousness came into her mother's eyes. She seemed about to say something else then changed her mind. "Now, what shall we do today?"

Chapter Three

The Grill Room of the Highland Inn was fashioned after an English pub with low-beamed ceilings, latticed amber windows, round tables and Windsor chairs. Along one side was a curved bar with high leather stools studded with brass nail heads. As Coryn and her parents entered, a heavyset man at the bar set down his drink and came over to Coryn's father.

"Bryson Falvey," the man said, holding out his large hand. "Falvey Heavy Equipment. We hear you're thinking of unseating old Mason Bigelow. That's good news." He pumped Neil's hand. "We need someone like you in Sacramento."

"Well, thank you. Very kind of you to say so. Nothing's definite yet…"

The man didn't seem to hear her father's words, just clapped him on the shoulder and went back to his seat at the bar.

When they were at their own table, Coryn asked

her father, "Are you seriously considering running for the assembly, Dad?"

"Several people are urging me to think about it. It's mostly talk. Nothing's been decided."

Coryn noticed her mother nervously rearranging silver at her plate. Didn't she like the idea?

Neil opened the glossy red menu. "Now, what would you ladies enjoy tonight? How about a nice sirloin, or fresh salmon fillet?"

The next few minutes were spent choosing their dinner entrées. Coryn's father exchanged a few friendly remarks with the waitress, who evidently knew him, then gave her their order.

When they were alone again, Neil looked at Coryn and picked up the conversation where they'd left off. "However, if I *did* decide to run, how about going to work for me on my campaign committee? With your PR experience, you could contribute a great deal. I'd pay you—match your salary in L.A. or more. And—" he laughed "— you wouldn't have any living expenses. Free room and board."

Coryn didn't have a chance to reply because the waitress came with their shrimp cocktails and her father did not return to the subject.

As soon as they got home, Clare told them she was going to take a long, leisurely bath and go to bed. Her father had some work to do and went to his den. Coryn went upstairs to her bedroom.

All through dinner she had felt restless. A couple of times she had completely lost track of the conversation. That hadn't mattered so much because several people had stopped by their table to engage her father in conversation. Over and over, the subject of his running for office had come up, but he had dismissed it lightly. It bothered Coryn that her mother had seemed so detached from it all. More than detached, she reflected, the subject seemed to make Clare anxious, though she did her best to hide it.

Coryn shut the door of her room and glared at the phone—the blue Princess one, her parents' gift to her on her fourteenth birthday. Her own line, her own number. She had been ecstatic.

She sat down on the side of the bed and stared at it. Maybe she'd just call her apartment in L.A., check the message machine. No harm in that. She heard the prerequisite six rings, the click of the recording machine. There was no message from Jason. Just her roommate Sheila's voice saying she'd gone to San Leandro to her folks' home for Thanksgiving.

Disappointed, Coryn put down the phone. Why hadn't Jason called from Detroit? She knew the name of the hotel where he said he'd be staying. It was one of the chain the company account executives used. She could call him there. What would be wrong with that? She could make it sound casual. Ask him how the sales presentation went. After all, they had discussed nothing else for weeks. They had brainstormed ideas together. He seemed to think some of hers were good. Had he used them? Wouldn't it seem natural she'd be interested to hear how his presentation had gone?

She picked up the receiver and dialed the long-distance number. As she waited, she caught a glimpse of herself in the dressing-table mirror. It brought a sudden flashback. She remembered how many nights she had glared at this same phone when she was a teenager, waiting for a certain boy to call. Ironic, ten years later, she was doing the same thing. Almost.

The hotel switchboard operator came on the line and Coryn asked to be connected to Jason Kramer's room.

The phone rang several times. Then, "Jason Kramer here." His voice sounded crisp, businesslike.

"Jason, it's Coryn. How did it go? I've been thinking about you and—" She stopped. She sounded overeager, gushy.

"Coryn. Oh, well. Yes, it went well." Was he annoyed or was that her imagination?

Coryn twisted the phone cord through her fingers. She hadn't meant to say it, but she gave in, couldn't stop herself. "Why didn't you call? Why didn't you let me know?"

She was sure she could hear someone moving around in the background. "Jason?" Coryn heard a distinctly feminine voice call.

She closed her eyes, drew a deep breath. Had she no pride?

She clutched the receiver, which slipped a little in her clammy palm.

"I told you I'd be busy here," he snapped.

She clenched her teeth. What was that she heard? Had he put his hand over the mouthpiece, was he speaking to someone there in the room with him? He came back on the line. He seemed a little impatient.

"I'll have to go, Coryn. There're some people I've got to meet downstairs in the lounge."

She waited, holding her breath a few seconds longer, idiotically, not wanting to hang up. Surely he would say something about her input. Tell her some of her ideas had helped?

Jason's voice came on again, a little bored. Indifferent? "I'll be in L.A. on the first. I'll call you then."

Her fingers tightened on the receiver. *No, you won't,* a voice in her head said.

There was definite irritation in Jason's tone now. "I better wrap this up, Coryn. I'll see you back in L.A."

Coryn did not answer. Slowly she put down the phone.

After she'd hung up, she sat perfectly still for a long time. Why had she been such a fool? Why hadn't she resisted the urge to call him. She had a feeling of finality. All her nagging doubts and questions about Jason came rushing for confirmation. Little cracks in his veneer had appeared months ago. She just hadn't wanted to see them. He was the reason she'd stayed in L.A. Long after she was bored with her job, disliked the life-style around her. She should have come home months ago when she first realized who and what Jason was.

The irrefutable truth descended like an icy cloak. Whatever she had felt for Jason or he for her was over. Whatever purpose she'd had in his life had been served. He didn't need her anymore. It was humiliating to admit. The truth might be best but it also could be ugly. She sat there perfectly still while her conviction took hold. She drew a long, shaky breath.

She wasn't going back to L.A.

She didn't want to face Jason. Or, everyone at the office. They would all know how he'd made a fool of her. Maybe they knew already, she grimly reflected.

Besides, she didn't care about that job. But if she didn't go back, what would she do? She'd figure that out later. Once that was decided, there were other things to do to make it stick. To make it so she couldn't change her mind.

First, she had to resign her job. That wouldn't cause any waves. It was an entry-level position. If she had potential, she could move up they'd told her. Her potential had been given to feeding Jason ideas for him to present. She'd never learned to be assertive enough. She'd trusted him to give her credit. It hadn't happened.

The following day when she made the call to the office it was as she'd expected. No one asked her many questions.

Next, she had to call Sheila to let her know she'd have to look for another roommate. That was a lot harder. But Sheila was a friend and very understanding. Good apartments at reasonable rents in safe neighborhoods were at a premium in L.A. Before she could allow herself to have any second thoughts she dialed Sheila at her parents' house, where she was visiting for the holiday.

Sheila was disappointed that Coryn wasn't coming back but surprised her by saying, "Actually, I think

I saw it coming. You've been so depressed. Sure, you did a good job of covering it, but I could see you'd lost your enthusiasm.''

"It was that obvious, huh?"

"Well, you know me," Sheila laughed. "I should hang out my shingle. Like Lucy in the Peanuts cartoon strip. 'The Doctor is In'." She laughed, "I guess you could say, I saw the handwriting on the wall."

"You did? Well, you were ahead of me. I just woke up." Coryn's voice was tinged with irony. There was a slight pause, then Sheila asked, "What about Jason?"

"What about him?"

"Does he know you're not coming back?"

"I told him."

"Is he the reason?"

"Partly."

"I hope you're okay about it."

"I can't discuss it right now. I'll fill you in another time, okay?"

"Sure." Sheila agreed. Then they'd launched into a discussion of the best way to send Coryn's belongings. The things she had purchased for their common use at the apartment—the iron and toaster, for instance—she told Sheila to keep. Her clothes were the main items that would have to be shipped.

"I'm sorry you have to do all this, Sheila. I know it's an awful lot to ask," Coryn said. "I feel I've let you down. I'll pay my part of next month's rent if you have trouble finding someone to share the apartment."

"No way."

Sheila assured her things could be worked out. She had lots of friends and was great at networking. Before they hung up Sheila said, "If you want my advice, which you probably don't, forget Jason Kramer. He isn't worth it."

"Thanks, Anne Landers."

Sheila's words reaffirmed what Coryn had concluded herself. Although forgetting Jason might be easier said than done. However, Coryn was determined to do it. He'd taken up too much of her time, energy, life already.

After she put the phone down Coryn just sat there. With two calls she had changed the direction of her life. Now what?

Even a bad experience can teach something if one is willing to learn. Maybe every woman has to have one disastrous romance in her life so that she can at least know what she doesn't want. The question in Coryn's heart was were her dreams of an enduring love too idealistic? Had she expected too much, trusted too much? Was there such a thing anymore as true love? Or did she cling to a hope that could never be fulfilled?

Chapter Four

Thanksgiving came as a welcome distraction. It took her mind off what she'd done. If she'd had time to think about it she might have regretted her impulsive decision. She was sure she'd been right about Jason. Breaking off would have eventually happened anyway. What bothered her was, now what? Not knowing the answer, helping her mother gave her a chance to put off making any immediate decisions about her future.

This year for Thanksgiving, besides Coryn's aunts, her father's two sisters and their husbands from Redding, her father's lawyer Martin Prentis and his wife Lucille, old time friends, several other local couples had been invited. When Coryn asked her mother why some of these were being included in what had always been a family occasion, the answer was, "Well, Neil wanted some of the people that are urging him to run for the assembly. Actually as a kind of courtesy.'' That was also the reason her mother gave for having the turkey and most of the trimmings catered.

"But what about your famous candied sweet potato casserole and creamed onions?'' asked Coryn in surprise. These were two of her mother's specialties.

"Oh, everyone's on a diet these days,'' was the offhanded reply. ''With the extra people Neil invited, it just seemed—'' she paused, ''I haven't been doing much entertaining lately...''

Coryn accepted the explanation. Preoccupied with her own new problems it sounded reasonable enough. She pitched in to help with some of the details of preparing for her parents' guests. These mainly consisted of polishing the silver, arranging the flowers, and creating a cornucopia of fruit as a centerpiece for the buffet table.

Coryn moved through the day itself as if playing a role, smiling, chatting, answering questions about her life in L.A. casually. She was glad when evening came and all the guests had left. It was only when she was alone in her own room that she then faced the decisions she had made, the steps she had taken and confronted what she would do next.

Thanksgiving morning Mark got up late. The day was gloomy and windy. The sky dark, heavy with clouds threatening rain. He got up, put on his bathrobe and slippers. As he passed through the living room, he flipped on the TV. In the kitchen he dumped some cornflakes into a bowl, then clicked on the automatic coffeemaker.

The sound of the TV blared and he went to turn

it down. The famous New York Thanksgiving Day parade was being telecast with its marching bands, floating air-balloon figures, baton twirlers and horseback riders. He watched for a few minutes, hoping the Bartons had turned it on for Ginny. She loved it. She recognized all the cartoon characters and called out their names, clapping her hands happily. His heart twisted. He missed her. Maybe he should have stayed in San Raphael with her, in spite of the memories.

The scene changed to a commercial and Mark went back out to the kitchen. His coffee was ready and he poured some into a mug. Gulping it, he stood staring out the window over the sink. It was beginning to rain. A gray steady rain that he knew would last all day.

Good thing there'd be marathon football. From California to Florida some of the biggest college teams would be playing. It would fill up the empty hours of this long day yawning ahead.

Noon found him still in his bathrobe in front of the TV, not knowing which team was even playing, which was winning or losing. Mindlessly watching the constantly moving figures on the screen, Mark's thoughts were far from points and scores.

He used the remote to change channels. Sleet fell heavily at the traditional Army-Navy game. The players battled through the soggy turf. Click, click. Sunshine in Florida. Click. In Michigan snow fell.

Mark's finger poised above the button, mesmerized by the picture of snow flurries. Snow. Always reminded him. How could it not? Squaw Valley nearly four years ago.

They'd been on one of their favorite vacations, their first since adopting Ginny. A ski weekend. It was wonderful. Ginny at two was fun, easy to take with them, enjoying everything. Shari was the skier. It was a sport she loved, and she was a good skier. Mark was a klutz on skis and had taken Ginny sledding so Shari could be free to run the slopes.

Then the unexpected, the unthinkable, happened. A freak accident. The ski lift broke, tumbling skiers thirty feet. Shari had hit her head and had been killed instantly.

A minute before, she had been laughing, waving down at him as he held Ginny in his arms. "Just one more time," she had pleaded when he suggested they call it a day, go back to the lodge. She had been having such a good time...

Click, click, Mark switched channels. Then he stood up, turned off the set. He looked out the window. A gray veil of rain darkened the afternoon. He turned abruptly and hurried to his bedroom, flinging off robe, pajamas as he did. Couldn't stay holed up like this another minute. Rain or no rain, he was going jogging. He pulled on his sweats, tied his running shoes and left the house.

Stepping outside on the porch, the cold, wet wind stung his face. He warmed up by running in place a few minutes, then set out through the misty rain.

An hour later he was back, blood tingling, muscles aching, but feeling better. After a long shower, he shoved a frozen pizza into the microwave and studied the TV listings. The movie channel was playing a John Wayne retrospective. *The Quiet Man* was scheduled next. Why not? Mark got the pizza out, put it on a tray and carried it into the living room and settled down in his easy chair. Some Thanksgiving, he thought with grim humor. Next year, it would be different. He'd make sure of it.

He settled back to lose himself in the movie. In two more days he'd go back to San Rafael, bring Ginny home and life would get back to normal.

Yet, it would never seem the same without Shari. Ginny needed a father *and* a mother.

For some reason, Coryn Dodge came into his mind. Her eyes, so clear and candid, yet still holding a kind of mystery. What was she really like when you got to know her? Mark had the impression there were layers to her personality. Things he would find interesting, intriguing, exciting. Not that he'd ever know. She was going back to L.A. after the holiday.

The morning after Thanksgiving Coryn awoke at seven. Her inner alarm clock working, she guessed, it was the time she usually got up to get ready to leave for the office.

It took her a few minutes to compute that she didn't have an office to go to, didn't have to fight the early-morning freeway traffic. L.A. and everything there was now history.

Tossing aside the covers, she got out of bed. Outside, early-morning fog swirled. She pulled on a sweater and an old pair of jeans she found in her closet and went out into the hall.

The house was quiet. On her way downstairs she passed her parents' closed bedroom door. They must be still asleep.

To her surprise her father was in the kitchen, making himself a cup of coffee, something she had rarely seen him do. He looked preoccupied. When he saw her, he lifted his eyebrows.

"You're up early. Thought you'd sleep in this morning after being up so late last night."

"I was awake. I thought I might as well get up," Coryn said. Ranger rose from his place under the table and, tail wagging like a metronome, came stiffly over to her. She rubbed his head, "Mornin', old fella."

"'Fraid you'll have to make coffee. I settled for instant," her father said. He glanced down at the newspaper on the table. "I've got an early meeting and didn't want to take the time."

"That's okay." She moved past him, got the canister of coffee down and started to measure it into the paper-filter cup. She gave him a curious look. He seemed on edge, as if something troubling was on his mind.

"By the way, Coryn, I haven't told you how glad I am you decided not to go back to L.A." He folded the paper and pushed it aside on the table. "I hope you won't try to get another job for a while. I was serious when I suggested you help with my campaign, if there is one. But aside from that, it would be nice for you to be here, keep your mother company. I think she gets pretty lonesome. Not good for her." He paused. "Your mother misses you, honey.

You know, the only chick, the empty nest syndrome. She'd love to have you home for a while. We both would.''

That her self-confident, self-absorbed father *needed* her had never occurred to Coryn before. That he would verbalize it caused a little pinch of anxiety.

Her father glanced at his watch, took a final sip of his coffee, then set down his coffee mug. ''Got to be off. Meeting at eight.'' He put his hand on her shoulder, kissed her cheek. ''Think about it, honey. We really love having you home.''

After her father left, Coryn felt puzzled. She thought of the subtle tension she had been aware of between him and her mother. Did he think her presence would act as a buffer somehow? Distracted by the thought, she plugged in the coffeemaker, and shoved two pieces of wholewheat bread into the toaster. While waiting, she stood at the sink staring out at the gloomy landscape. Wind tossed the limbs of the tall pines in a wild dance against the pewter sky. She had forgotten how long, dreary Rockport winters could be and suddenly felt depressed. Sometimes she had also been depressed in L.A. sunshine. So how she felt had nothing to do with the weather. Rather, she had shut one door of her life, slammed it actually, and she couldn't see another door to enter yet. The sound of the toast popping up diverted her attention. Enough of this, she told herself, as she buttered it. She'd read somewhere that physical activity was the best antidote for depression. As soon as she'd had some coffee she would take a walk.

Still, she couldn't shake the conviction that something was wrong here. Terribly wrong. Maybe this was just some sort of temporary phase. She'd noticed her mother's reaction to that Falvey man talking to her father about running for the assembly. Maybe they'd disagreed over the possibility of his going into politics. Whatever it was, it was upsetting the usual smooth surface of the Dodges' home.

A walk, that's what she needed. A long walk. She took down her jacket from the peg near the back door and put it on. Ranger's tail began to thump. His leash hung on one of the other pegs. All she had ever had to do was rattle it and Ranger was up and ready to go.

"Want to go, fella?" Coryn asked, automatically reaching for the leash. Ranger tried to get to his feet, slipped on the vinyl floor. He sank back down, put his muzzle between his front paws, looked up at Coryn, as if to say, *Sorry, these old bones won't take me where I used to run.*

Coryn replaced the leash, stooped down to caress the dog affectionately, kiss the top of his head. "It's okay, boy. Another time."

Outside it was damp with the chill of a typical north-coast winter day. Hands deep in her flannel-lined pockets, head bent against the wind, Coryn quickened her pace. Gradually, new energy kicked in. She felt a tingling sensation in her arms and legs. Her heart rate increased.

She walked on mindlessly in the chill air, paying little attention to where she was going. Fog dripped from the tall Douglas firs along the way, she felt it beading her scarf. She tugged up the collar of her jacket, looked around. She had come much farther than she had meant to, preoccupied with thoughts that tumbled like a child's alphabet blocks, the numbers and letters on them making no sense. She stopped, shivering with cold, to get her bearings. She had walked out of the familiar residential area into an older section of town. In the distance, through the fog, she saw the blurry lights of a neon sign spelling out the words Al's Diner. It had been a favorite hangout in her teen years. She was about two blocks from the high school. She hurried toward the diner. She decided a cup of hot coffee would warm her up for the homeward trek.

The air inside the diner was steamy, thick with the smell of frying bacon and sausage from the grill. She ordered a coffee at the counter then slipped into one of the red-vinyl booths.

The waitress brought the coffee in a thick white mug, set it down in front of her and whipped out an order pad. "Our special today is potato pancakes or apple turnovers with sausage."

Coryn stared at the woman for a stunned moment. It was like being in a time warp. The same red V-shaped apron and headband. She must be a hundred years old. Hadn't she worked here when Coryn was in high school?

The waitress waited, her pencil poised. "So which will it be?"

Coryn shook her head and said, "Just this coffee, thanks."

The waitress looked a little offended then went off, pocketing her order pad.

Still feeling somewhat dazed, Coryn wrapped both hands around the mug to warm them and cautiously took a sip of the scalding-hot coffee.

"Coryn."

Hearing her name made her jump. She set down the mug, spilling a little, and looked up, right into Mark Emery's warm brown eyes.

"Sorry, I didn't mean to startle you." He stood beside her table. "I was just surprised to see you. I mean, I thought you were going back to L.A. after Thanksgiving."

"That's okay. It was just that I was sort of spaced out." She mopped up the spill with the edge of a paper napkin.

"May I join you? Or would you rather be alone?"

"No. I mean, fine. Please do."

Mark slid into the seat opposite her. "I always stop here to get coffee to go and a doughnut to take to the office with me. I was surprised to see you here."

"This used to be an old high-school haunt. I was out walking, and just thought I'd drop in to warm up."

He opened the top of the plastic coffee container he'd been holding and spooned in some sugar from the dispenser. He stirred his coffee for a minute while looking across the table at her.

Even at this early hour, Coryn Dodge looked undeniably attractive. Her eyes bright, her skin glowing from the outdoor exercise.

"I thought you'd be back in L.A. by now."

Coryn shook her head. "Not yet. I'm staying through Christmas. Maybe longer. It depends."

Her vague answer seemed to puzzle him. He gave her a quizzical look, then said, "I'm afraid I have disturbed you."

"Not at all," she quickly protested.

"You sure? You seem..."

"I'm sorry. I guess I was just doing some heavy thinking. Not advisable this early in the morning." She gave a small laugh. "I guess if I decide to stay in Rockport, I have to figure out what I'll do. I'll have to find a job of some kind. I don't even know where to look. This town has changed a great deal since I lived here."

"For the better?"

"I don't know. I'm not sure. It seems like I've been away for a long time. At least it feels that way.

"Meaning L.A. is light years from Rockport." He sounded amused but his eyes were sympathetic. "It does take getting used to. But I'm finding I like the slower pace, the laid-back life-style."

Mark checked his watch. "Gotta run. I've an appointment out in Field's Landing. I'm doing a feature on seniors. It's turned out to be fascinating. Each person I've interviewed is different. Some regard old age as the end, while others are like kids, enthusiastic, looking forward, trying new things." Mark shook his head. "Funny, some people are old at fifty, others young at eighty." Mark took a final sip of his coffee and stood up. "It was nice seeing you again. Now that you're staying, maybe we'll see each other again."

"It's a possibility." She smiled. "It's a small town."

He smiled then, too. A smile that brought a warm light to his deep brown eyes and caused Coryn's pulse to quicken. Then, with a wave of his hand, he was gone.

Coryn remained a few minutes thinking about the coincidence of running into Mark so soon after their encounter in San Francisco. It *was* a small world. Chances are they would see each other somewhere again. That is if she *really* decided to stay in Rockport.

She left the diner and started back toward home. So many jumbled thoughts crowded into her mind. She knew she had made the right decision about Jason. That wasn't what troubled her. What she should do next was the problem. Her father's words this morning *had* bothered her. There was something beneath his casual suggestion that she stay home for a while. But what?

Her parents had always seemed completely content together. In fact, sometimes she had even felt they didn't need anyone else—not even *her*—to be happy. The ideal couple. That's how she had always thought of them. That's why it seemed so odd—Coryn brushed aside the worrying thoughts that crept back. Was her parents' perfect marriage coming apart?

She turned in the driveway and saw the kitchen light was on and her mother was standing at the window. When she saw Coryn she smiled and waved. Coryn waved back, feeling reassured. Maybe she had let her imagination run away with her. Everything was fine. Just as it had always been.

December

Chapter Five

Coryn's parents expressed their satisfaction that she had given up her job in L.A. and decided to remain in Rockport.

"At least until after the first of the year," she said cautiously not wanting to make any promise she couldn't keep. "I have many things to figure out."

They accepted that without comment whatever they secretly hoped she might decide to do.

"Oh, it will be marvelous having you here for Christmas," her mother said. "I do think you should call Cindy and make some plans since you're going to be here longer than you thought."

So the first week of December, heeding her mother's urging, Coryn finally called her childhood friend Cindy Barnes, now Cindy Lowell. There was no excuse for not letting people know she was back in Rockport. At least temporarily.

"Coryn, how great!" Cindy exclaimed when Coryn called to make a date for lunch. "Lora will be so excited. You can't imagine how often we talk about you. About all the things the three of us used to do."

"There's a lot to catch up on," Coryn answered, "Where shall we meet?"

"There's a new restaurant in Old Town I've been dying to try, the Seafarer. Tuesday's best for me. That's Benjy's day at nursery school. I'll contact Lora so she can work on getting a sitter."

Hearing this Coryn remembered with a shock that her two best friends were now mothers. Of course, she'd sent baby gifts. But she'd almost forgotten. The people she knew in L.A. were mostly single.

"Can't wait to see you," Cindy said gaily before she hung up.

Suddenly Coryn had mixed feelings about the upcoming reunion. She wasn't sure if she really wanted to stroll down memory lane. Would she feel completely out of touch? Would the three of them, who once were so close, have much in common after all this time? Would it feel strange now that their lives were so different? Well, it was too late to worry about that.

Old Town had once been a run-down waterfront area, lined with derelict buildings, empty storefronts with broken windows, seedy bars and dilapidated Victorian houses in various degrees of decay. Most people had avoided walking along the grim streets even in broad daylight, afraid of being panhandled by disheveled drunks, or confronted by loudly arguing tavern patrons standing outside the dingy entrances.

About six years earlier, a group of civic-minded merchants, retailers, businessmen and city officials decided to clean up Old Town. They'd transformed it by turning what was already there into tourist-attractive places. They'd restored, renovated, repaired the buildings, leaving their unique architecture intact. The streets with brick walkways and old-fashioned lampposts established a nineteenth-century atmosphere. Boutiques, bookstores, toy shops, art galleries, restaurants, all conforming to the theme, gradually opened. Soon shoppers and tourists were flocking to Old Town.

During the pre-Christmas season, Old Town was a magic place. Uniquely trimmed Christmas trees stood in front of every shop and store. Swags of evergreen and twists of laurel leaves studded with bunches of bright red holly berries, draped from lamppost to lamppost. From the gazebo in the center of Old Town, a carillon played Christmas music, lifting spirits into the holiday mood and motivating shoppers to even more gift buying.

An old-fashioned horse and carriage with a driver dressed in appropriate garb provided an authentic Dickensian touch to the scene.

The Seafarer was one of the newer restaurants, decorated with nostalgic touches of the 1800s. On the walls were framed photographs of early woodsmen standing proudly on huge felled timber, and of the large cargo ships that used to sail into Rockport Bay when it was a thriving seaport of fishing boats, their nets bulging with their catch. Bentwood chairs were placed at round tables covered with red-checked cloths. Baskets of ferns hung at the windows, which offered scenic views of the wharf. This had become the favorite eatery for women shoppers and it was always busy.

Cindy and Lora were already seated when Coryn arrived after leaving her mother at the beauty salon. Both women greeted her warmly and rose to give her hugs, declaring she looked wonderful.

"It's that Beverly Hills touch." Lora sighed dramatically.

"Definitely," Cindy agreed, laughing. "So tell us all about life in the fast track."

"Hardly life in the fast track," she said. "Fighting freeway traffic, work, frozen dinners..."

"Oh, come on! Surely there's some glitter in all this!" Cindy looked skeptical. "A man?"

"No one special," Coryn said, and knew it was now true. She was glad the waitress came to take their order.

Decisions were made with much ado about dieting and calorie counting, exchange of quotes from the health-food-nut instructor of the aerobics class they were taking.

Finally, the patient waitress left with their menus and the conversation immediately turned to reminiscing. Coryn felt herself drifting off from the conversation. She couldn't remember half the things they were recalling. If she stayed in Rockport, would she fit in again? The only one of the trio, not married?

Could she find a place here again, a life-style that would work?

Coryn looked at her two friends. The three of them had grown up together, sleeping over at one another's homes nearly every weekend, sharing dates, proms, opinions. They had been secure in their friendship. One by one they had paired off, gone steady, fallen in love. The spring they had all graduated college she had been a bridesmaid in both weddings. That summer, she had gone to L.A.

Their seafood salads were served and they chatted about mutual friends and whatever-happened-to-so-and-so. The waitress reappeared and rattled off the day's list of delectable dessert possibilities. Reluctantly they passed on it.

"I feel so virtuous I think we should go shopping," Cindy declared, laughing.

"Sure, why not?" Lora agreed as she got out her compact to freshen her lipstick. "I've got a sitter for the rest of the afternoon."

Lora glanced at Coryn, "How about you? It's not Rodeo Drive but they do have some new stores at the mall."

Coryn checked her watch. She had more than an hour to spare before she was supposed to meet her mother. Yet, she didn't want to extend the visit with her old girlfriends a minute longer. "I'm sorry, I can't join you this time," Coryn said. "I'm meeting Mom after her hair appointment. I promised I'd help her Christmas shop, she has a list a yard long."

"She does?" Cindy looked surprised. "That's funny, I ran into your mom in October. I remember because I was getting Halloween things for the kids. She joked about having nearly all her Christmas shopping done.''

"That's another thing I always admired about your mother, Coryn,'' Lora commented. "Besides being gorgeous. She was always so organized, on top of things.''

Coryn felt a small flutter in her stomach. That was the reputation her mother had. But since she'd been at home, there had been a series of incidents that troubled Coryn. Sometimes Clare seemed vague, forgetful, confused. Doing things like leaving the stove burners turned on, as her father had pointed out. And there had been other things. For a moment, she considered what Lora had just said. Something kept her from making the glib comments she might have given ordinarily.

Coryn left the Seafarer with a sense of relief. She said goodbye to the other two, making some noncommittal remarks about getting together again. As she walked in the direction of the beauty salon her mother patronized, she saw a man and a little girl coming toward her. As they got closer, she saw the man was Mark Emery. The child with him must be his daughter.

They saw each other almost at the same time. She looked as surprised as he was. Coryn Dodge was even prettier than he remembered. In sunlight her hair had mahogany lights, her blue eyes seemed bluer. She was dressed in a blazer, pants, a silk scarf patterned with vivid autumn leaves was knotted casually at her neck.

"Hello there," he greeted her. "What a wonderful surprise." The warm look in his eyes made her heart skip a beat.

Coryn smiled. "Good to see you again, Mark."

He turned to the little girl beside him, "Coryn, I'd like you to meet Ginny. Ginny, this lady is Coryn Dodge. We came up on the same plane from San Francisco after I left you at Nana's and Grampa's."

The child regarded Coryn with wide curious eyes. She had a spray of golden freckles across a small button nose and round, rosy cheeks.

Coryn held out her hand. "I'm happy to meet you, Ginny."

Ginny smiled, shook Coryn's hand. She was not at all shy, but she had a sweetness about her that suggested the security of being well-loved.

"Are you Christmas shopping?" Coryn asked.

"Sort of." Ginny glanced at Mark, as if for confirmation. "We shopped for the Three Wise Men."

Puzzled, Coryn looked first at Mark then back at Ginny.

"See, first we got the stable scene, where the Baby Jesus was born, and the angels. Last year, we got the shepherds and some of the sheep. So *this* year we get the Three Kings," Ginny explained.

"Shari, Ginny's mother, always wanted Ginny to understand Christmas wasn't just presents and Santa Claus, so we started celebrating 'little Christmas,' too. January sixth commemorating the arrival of the Magi."

"How lovely," Coryn said, touched by this unique family custom. "So, did you find them?"

"Yes, they're great! They've got crowns and gold-trimmed robes and all." Ginny smiled happily. "Now we're going for a carriage ride, aren't we, Daddy?"

Mark nodded. "A promise is a promise."

"That should be fun."

The carriage was just turning the corner at the end of the street. It came to a stop a few yards from where they were standing. As the driver helped down the couple who had been riding, Mark raised his hand to signal that they wanted to hire the carriage next. Coryn walked over to the curb with them.

Ginny gave a little skip, swinging Mark's hand, then she glanced up at Coryn. "Want to come with us?"

The driver stepped forward and said with a grin, "Same price, one or two adults with a child."

"How about it?" Mark asked Coryn. "Would you like to?"

Riding in a carriage with Mark and Ginny would certainly beat waiting in a beauty salon for her mother, she thought. "Why not?" she replied with a smile. "How long will it take?"

"Fifteen minutes is the ride, miss." The driver tipped his stovepipe hat, opened the carriage door.

Coryn looked at Mark, Ginny and the carriage. It did look like fun. "Okay, I'd love to."

The next thing she knew, she was being helped up into the carriage. With a flick of the driver's whip, they started off. Coryn glanced at Mark. He looked different this afternoon. Younger, handsomer, his hair was tousled by the brisk wind off the bay. He was wearing a creamy Irish-knit sweater, corduroy pants. He was obviously more relaxed and enjoyed being with his child.

The horses' hooves clip-clopped on the brick streets as they rolled through Old Town. People walking along the sidewalks looked at them, smiled and waved. Ginny giggled.

"Let's wave back like the English royals I've seen on TV!" Coryn suggested. She fluttered her hand in the famous back-hand wave Queen Elizabeth gave while riding in *her* carriage.

"Yes! Let's!" said Ginny as she bounced happily and followed suit.

Mark looked a little embarrassed, but grinned indulgently at both of them.

The wind was strong, cold. Coryn pulled her silk scarf from around her neck and tied it under her chin to keep her hair from blowing into her face.

Coryn enjoyed the ride thoroughly. Seeing Rockport from the vantage of a carriage was like being transported back in time. She glanced at Mark, smiling. "This is *really* fun!"

He grinned back. Coryn *was* having a good time. Her eyes were sparkling, and her smile—why, she looked really beautiful.

They went up Viewmont Hill to its crest, where Highland Inn stood, then back, and circled the little park in the center of Old Town. The driver shouted "Whoa!" to his compliant horse, and pulled to a stop.

Ginny looked disappointed.

"It was too short, wasn't it?" Coryn said understandingly.

"Well, maybe we'll do it again," Mark said, getting out, then turned back to lift Ginny down. "But now we're going for our treat, remember?"

"Oh, yes! We're going to have a frozen-yogurt cone," Ginny told Coryn. "Pumpkin flavor. It's my favorite."

"For the time being, right?" Mark laughed. "Would you like to come with us?"

Coryn again glanced at her watch and hesitated. She still had a half hour before she had arranged to meet her mother. She would like to stretch this time with Mark Emery and his little girl longer. She made up her mind quickly, "Okay, I will. A frozen-yogurt cone sounds just great!"

With perfect naturalness, Ginny took Coryn's hand and the three of them walked down the street together to Old Town's Old Fashioned Ice Cream Parlor. On the way Ginny chattered happily. The pink-and-white-striped awnings outside the shop matched the ruffled aprons and headbands on the girls behind the counter. Inside, the decor was so deliberately nostalgic, with curlicued metal chairs and faux-marble-top round tables that Coryn and Mark exchanged an amused look. But it was also charming and since Ginny was enjoying herself completely, their amusement remained shared but unspoken.

Ginny had a little trouble with the generous double-dip serving. The creamy substance melted away faster than her small tongue could lick it up. Ginny fretted a bit as it started to drip down the side of the cone and onto her hands, but Coryn quickly came to the rescue. She took some packaged handi-wipes from her purse and she deftly cleaned Ginny's chin and sticky fingers.

"You must have been a Girl Scout. Always prepared." Mark commented, his eyes amused. Coryn smiled.

"I'm going to be a Brownie. Next year when I'm seven," announced Ginny.

Coryn saw the look of tenderness on Mark's face and was touched. It was clear he adored his little girl.

Coryn checked her watch again and said, "Sorry, but I have to hurry. I really do need to meet up with my mother." She got up to leave, "Thanks for inviting me to your party. I really enjoyed myself."

Their gazes met. Mark smiled and she caught her breath.

"We enjoyed having you along," Mark told her.

"It was fun waving in the carriage," Ginny added.

They said goodbye and Coryn hurried away in the opposite direction. She felt happy and lighthearted. Meeting up with Mark and his child had been a most pleasant surprise. She liked what she'd seen. He was a real hands-on Daddy.

As Mark and Ginny came out of the ice-cream parlor and were walking back down the street, they were hailed by the driver who was standing by his mount and carriage waiting for customers.

"Sir! The lady forgot her scarf," the carriage driver said, handing Mark the length of silk. Mark took it, held it for a second, breathing in the scent that clung to it. He recognized it. It was the same distinctive perfume he had noticed the night he had driven her home from the airport.

"It's pretty, isn't it, Daddy?" Ginny asked, fingering the edge of the scarf. "Like Coryn. She's pretty, too, isn't she?"

"Yes, very," Mark answered, folding the scarf and putting it in his jacket pocket. "She'll be sorry she lost it. We'll have to return it to her, won't we?"

Chapter Six

Coryn stepped inside LaMode Beauty Salon and was immediately swept into a pink perfumed world. The assorted fragrances of lotions, cosmetics and shampoo mingled in the warm air. Blow-dryers whirred and women's voices murmured. A constant hum of conversation flowed from the pink-leather quilted booths and manicure tables.

A high-fashioned coiffeured blonde with vividly blue-shadowed eyes and incredible long, curved false eyelashes sat behind the reception desk. She was new since Coryn had last been here, and when Coryn asked if her mother was finished, the young woman ran long sequin-lacquered fingernails down the page of her open appointment book.

"Mrs. Dodge? Oh, yes. Are you her daughter? Well, she left a little while ago."

"Are you sure? I was to meet her here."

"I'll ask Justine, her stylist. But I'm almost certain…I'll find out,'' she said, and got up and moved into one of the nearby booths.

Coryn recognized the woman who followed the receptionist back to the desk as her mother's regular hairstylist.

''Hi, Coryn. Your mom wasn't feeling so well when we finished and I called a cab to take her home. She left her keys and said you could drive her car home.'' With her free hand she dug into her pink nylon smock pocket, brought out a set of keys and gave them to Coryn. ''Has your mom been sick? I didn't think she looked good when she came in…pale, sort of shaky. I thought maybe she'd had flu or was coming down with it.''

''I don't know. I hope not,'' Coryn said.

Justine tapped the hairbrush she was holding against her palm. ''Lately she's seemed…I don't know…not quite herself.''

Hearing someone else put into words what Coryn had felt about her mother since coming home made her suddenly tense. ''Thanks, Justine. I'll go right home and see how she is.''

Coryn drove home quickly, her heart beating hard, her breathing shallow. Something was wrong with her mother. But what?

She didn't know what prompted her to do it. But when she pulled into the garage, before going into the house, she unlocked the trunk of the car. Inside she found two large shopping bags filled with beautifully wrapped Christmas packages. The tags bore the same names of the friends and relatives her mother had put on her list to buy gifts for that very morning at the breakfast table.

But when had her mother bought these gifts? She'd been in the beauty parlor all morning, Coryn realized. She must have purchased the gifts days ago—and forgotten.

After staring at the presents for a few stunned minutes, Coryn slammed down the trunk and went into the house.

Rita, their weekly housecleaner, was vacuuming in the living room. In a hushed tone of voice she told Coryn her mother was napping.

"How did she look when she came home?" Coryn asked.

Rita frowned, leaned on the vacuum handle. "Not good. When I seen the cab pull up front, I looked out the window, not expecting anyone since you both were gone. Then I saw your mom come up the walk, ever so slow. I went right to the door and opened it. 'Mrs. Dodge, you look beat and that's for sure,' I told her. She said something about not feeling well, so I helped her up to her bedroom. She said she'd be all right if she'd just lie down for a bit. I took her up a cup of tea later but she had a cloth over her eyes and was just stretched out on the bed. I pulled the quilt over her and just tiptoed out." Rita shook her head. "Never saw her look that bad before."

"Maybe it's the flu," Coryn said through stiff lips, fearing it was something much worse than that.

Still shaken by the discovery of the Christmas presents in the car, Coryn went upstairs. She opened her mother's closed bedroom door, peeked in, saw she was sleeping and went on into her own.

What should she do? Ask her mother about the wrapped gifts, tagged and ready to give? Could her mother possibly have forgotten? She seemed to forget so many things these days.

Was something seriously wrong with her? All sorts of possibilities crowded into Coryn's mind. Some kind of emotional break? Some kind of amnesia?

She still hadn't decided whether to bring up the subject an hour later when her mother emerged from her bedroom, refreshed and fragrant from her rest and bath. She seemed perfectly fine. The explanation she gave for leaving the beauty salon early seemed perfectly logical.

"I should have eaten something before I went there. I rushed around shopping and then—it was so hot in there with all the steam and the smells of nail polish and blow-dryers going, I just felt faint. I didn't want to spoil your luncheon with Cindy and Lora, so it was simpler for me to come home in a cab."

Momentarily Coryn felt better. That evening, even with Coryn's observation, her mother seemed her usual self. They watched TV together, a Christmas program. It was like a hundred other evenings Coryn remembered at home. But she couldn't forget those packages in the trunk of the car. There *was* something going on here she didn't understand. But what?

Chapter Seven

The next afternoon Coryn helped her mother with the holiday ritual of baking dozens of sugar cookies. Clare was in a holiday mood, full of plans for Christmas. Her mother loved Christmas, everything about it, gave dozens of presents to people Coryn did not even know. She decided not to ask her about the gifts in the car. It didn't seem that important right now. Just as long as her mother was happy.

Wasn't it enough that her father was sometimes short with Clare? Reminding her of errands, phone calls, questioning her. Coryn saw how upset this made her mother. She considered asking her father about Clare's forgetfulness, but she knew the conversation would disturb him. It could even make things worse between them and she just didn't want to add to her mother's distress. She'd just let it go. For now.

As Clare slid the baked cookies off the sheet onto

the wax paper on the counter, the doorbell chimed, and she looked up. "Who could that be?"

"I'll go see, Mom."

When she opened the front door, Mark Emery and Ginny stood on the doorstep. "Why, hello."

"We just stopped by to bring you this." Mark held out her scarf. "You left it in the carriage yesterday."

"How kind of you. I didn't miss it." She took it. "Thank you."

Clare had followed her from the kitchen and was standing a little distance behind her. "Mom, I'd like you to meet Mark Emery and his little girl, Ginny. Mark, this is my mother, Clare Dodge."

"Well, I'm delighted to meet you, Mark. We read your byline regularly. My husband thinks you're doing a great job." Coryn's mother stepped forward, held out her hand to Mark. Then she looked down at Ginny. "And this is Ginny. Do come in, won't you? We've just been baking Christmas cookies. You can be our taste testers."

"Oh, I don't know, Mrs. Dodge. We wouldn't want to—"

Ginny tugged on Mark's hand, her upturned face eager.

"You won't be. Not at all. Come on in," Clare urged.

Coryn opened the door wider for them to enter.

"Here, let me take off your coat, Ginny, and you come along out to the kitchen with me," Clare said. "The little bell on the oven is about to ring that tells us the next batch is ready to take out. Then you can help decorate them, would you like that?"

The bonding was almost immediate. Ginny seemed to feel perfectly at ease with Coryn's mother. Without a backward look at her father, Ginny went down the hall to the kitchen with Clare, the two chatting like old friends.

Mark shook his head in wonder. "That's amazing. Ginny's not shy, but I've never seen her take to someone that quickly."

"My mother's always had a magic touch with children. All my friends adored her."

"She seems to be one of those rare people who has somehow managed to retain enough of the best elements of childhood so she can relate to children without talking down to them."

"Like Glynda, the Good Witch, in the *Wizard of Oz?* When I used to watch it on TV every year, I always thought my mother looked exactly like her." Coryn smiled, remembering what a magical childhood her mother had given her.

Mark grinned. "She does, sort of, doesn't she?"

"Here, let me take your jacket." Coryn took it and hung it up beside Ginny's little red parka. "Let's join them. Are you good at decorating cookies?"

"It's a skill I haven't really acquired."

"There's always a first time." She smiled again.

By the time they got to the kitchen, Coryn's mother had tied an apron around Ginny's neck. It covered her completely. A high stool at the kitchen counter provided her easy access to a number of small glass containers filled with tinted sugar, raisins, jellied candies and chocolate sprinkles. Coryn's mother then placed a tray of freshly-baked cookies in front of her.

"Look, Daddy, what I'm doing. See?" Her little hands moved swiftly. Tiny fingers curved delicately as she used them to dip into the various toppings. "This one's going to be a Christmas tree, so I'll use the green sugar and..." She went on happily talking, intent on the task at hand.

Coryn's mother was beside her, gently coaching but letting Ginny do the selecting and actual decorating. Coryn thought how happy she looked and was glad she hadn't mentioned the packages in the car. She saw Mark glance in the direction of her mother and Ginny as the animated chatting continued at the counter. An expression of tender amusement gave his strong-featured face a softness she hadn't noticed before. What a wonderful father he must be.

Just then the kitchen phone rang and her mother asked, "Will you get it, dear? My hands are all gooey." She held them up, wiggling her fingers.

Coryn picked up the phone, listened for a few minutes then said, "Just a minute, please." Holding the receiver against her shoulder she mouthed, "It's Mrs. Prentis, Mom. Something about the Christmas Tea at the club."

Mrs. Dodge made a little face, then whispered, "All right, I'll take it in the other room. Okay, honey?" she turned to the little girl. "I'll be back as soon as I can," she said as she left the room.

Coryn replaced the receiver then moved over to the counter, taking her mother's place beside Ginny. Ginny's face had a smudge of flour on both cheeks but she was smiling happily. "You come, too, Daddy!" she motioned to Mark.

"I don't know—" Mark shook his head.

"Yes you can, Daddy, I'll show you," Ginny urged.

"Come on, Mark, like the Little Red Hen, if you don't help you don't get to taste!" Coryn teased, winking at Ginny.

"That's right, Daddy." Ginny giggled.

There were lots of laughs and comments as Mark began to clumsily form the dough, use a cookie cutter to stamp out various shapes then decorate them. Urged on by Ginny he made clown faces and sprinkled colored sugar with abandon. The effects were greeted with enthusiastic praise by Ginny and Coryn.

"I may have missed my calling." Mark grinned as their batch of a dozen cookies was placed in the oven.

By the time Coryn's mother returned they were done and the baked results were viewed. Mark looked dubious as Ginny renewed her compliments. "I don't know. Mine get mixed reviews, I'm afraid."

"Never mind. They all taste the same." Coryn's mother comforted him. "We've got enough batter for another batch. So Ginny and I will finish up on these. Maybe you could make us some tea to have with them, Coryn?"

While Coryn put the kettle on to boil, got out cups and saucers, she asked Mark to choose the kind of tea from an assortment in a glass jar on the counter.

As Coryn poured some milk into a small ceramic creamer she saw Mark glance in the direction of her mother and Ginny as their cookie decorating and animated chatting continued at the counter.

"Your mother's awfully kind," he said, smiling at her.

"She loves children," Coryn said, then asked, "How is it you're not at the paper this time of day?"

"Ginny had an appointment with the optometrist so I took off some time to take her."

"I hope it's not anything serious. Does she have to wear glasses?"

"I don't think so. The school nurse noticed something while doing routine testing. She suggested a doctor should look at Ginny's eyes. She has something called a lazy eye." He lowered his voice, "She'll probably have to wear a patch over it a couple of days a week until it strengthens itself. The doctor gave me some stuff to read that explains the condition in layman's terms. Which I haven't had a chance to do yet."

The sound of laughter from the other two broke into their conversation. Coryn's mother called gaily, "Your daughter has a great sense of humor, Mr. Emery."

"I know, and please call me Mark, Mrs. Dodge."

"All right, I shall. Are you ready for these delicious and artistically decorated creations?" She slipped down from her stool and brought a plate of cookies over to the table. Ginny jumped down and ran over, too.

Ginny seemed so proud of her handiwork, Coryn found her sweet expression touching as she pointed out the cookies she'd decorated. "Oh, my—these are too beautiful to eat," Coryn told her. The little girl flushed with pleasure at the compliment.

The cookies were sampled and complimented lavishly. Then they were eaten along with the tea and a glass of milk for Ginny.

When Mark finally said they'd have to leave, Clare insisted Ginny select a dozen cookies to take home. Coryn put them in a plastic bag for her to carry.

Coryn walked to the door with them. In the front hall, Mark held Ginny's parka for her, zipped it up, then handed her a knitted cap saying, "Thanks for a great time."

"And for the cookies." Ginny held up the bag, smiling.

"You did a wonderful job decorating," Coryn told her.

"So did *you*. I liked your Christmas tree the best." Ginny said.

"Thank you." Coryn looked over Ginny's head and met Mark's amused expression.

He took Ginny's hand and said, "Well, thanks again."

As he started out the door, Coryn said, "By the way, Mark, we always have an open house on New Year's Day starting around five. Stop by if you're free."

Seeming surprised, Mark halted and then said, "Why, thank you very much."

As she closed the door behind them Coryn wondered, *would* he come? She realized she hoped he would. She would like to see Mark Emery again.

Chapter Eight

"Coryn! Wake up, dear."

Her mother's voice and her hand gently shaking her shoulder roused Coryn from a deep slumber. Coryn sat up, blinking sleepily. When she saw her mother standing by the side of her bed, she came immediately wide-awake. Clare was deathly pale, deep shadows circled her eyes, her expression was pained.

"Mom! What's wrong?"

"I'm sorry to waken you, dear, but I have a beastly headache, probably a migraine. The medicine, the only one that touches this kind, is starting to have some effect, but it will keep me in bed for most of the day, I'm afraid. That's why I had to wake you up. I need to ask a favor."

"Sure, Mom, anything. An ice bag for your head? Some tea?"

"No, thanks, dear. Nothing like that. I'll just have to sleep this off for a couple of hours. What I need you to do is go to the church in my place. I volunteered to help pack Christmas baskets for the needy.''

Coryn reached for her robe, threw back the covers and searched for her slippers.

"Of course, Mom. What time should I be there?"

"At ten. It's just a little after nine now."

"I can make that. I'll jump in the shower and be ready in a jiff. Are you sure there isn't something I can do for you before I leave?"

Her mother shook her head. "No, dear, that's all. That relieves me. I dislike not fulfilling a commitment. It's such a worthy cause and so few show up to do the job. I hate to let them down. Now that you're going, I can rest easy. Thank you, Coryn,'' she said as she left the room.

"No problem, Mom."

Coryn showered quickly, dressed in sweater, slacks. She peeked in her mother's bedroom before she went downstairs and saw her lying with an eye mask on, already asleep. Good. In the past, Clare occasionally had this sort of debilitating headache, but Coryn didn't recall ever seeing her look that bad. Could something more serious be the cause? Coupled with some of the other things she'd noticed about her mother, Coryn couldn't help worrying. A slow-growing tumor? That could account for some of it. Heavens, but she hoped it was nothing as serious as that! Only a headache, she assured herself.

In the kitchen she drank some juice and poured herself a cup of coffee. Then took her mother's car keys off the peg where she kept them and went out to the garage.

Good Shepherd Church was only a short drive. Her mother was a faithful member of the congregation. Coryn had gone to Sunday school here and had belonged to the youth group in high school. At college Coryn had gone to chapel service but in the last few years she had not regularly attended church. Certainly not in L.A. There, Sundays were usually spent around the pool of their apartment complex or at brunch parties that had become a trendy way to entertain. As she pulled into a space in the parking lot, Coryn felt a little guilty, like the black sheep turning up at the fold.

There were four ladies already working in the parish hall when Coryn entered. They looked at her curiously as she came in the door. Then one, a stout, gray-haired woman with sparkling brown eyes and a generous smile, greeted her, "Why, it's Coryn Dodge, isn't it? Hello there, I'm Mildred McCurry." She came over, both hands extended. "Your mother called earlier to say you'd be coming." Then she said sympathetically, "I hope she'll be feeling better. Those headaches are awful."

She took Coryn by the arm and led her over to a long table where the other volunteers were working and introduced her. They were busy filling baskets from cardboard cartons filled with canned food, bakery goods, boxes of cereal and dry milk, bags of flour and other groceries.

"You can work beside me, Coryn," Mrs. McCurry told her. "I'll show you the order in which we pack the baskets, staples on the bottom, crushables and perishables on top. Later, we check our lists. Families with children get a few extras, little toys, candy, some special sort of treat.''

Coryn took off her jacket, hung it up and got to work.

It was slow going at first, moving down the table following instructions as to what and how much went into each basket. She soon caught on and got into the rhythm. She had been working steadily for some time when one of the ladies called, "Break time." The smell of fresh coffee permeated the room and someone had set up a delicious buffet lunch for the workers.

"One thing about working for the church, you always get fed!" joked Mrs. McCurry.

"It's scriptural even," declared a lady Coryn had been introduced to as Emily Austin. "Cast your bread on the water and it returns to you buttered."

"Emily!" remonstrated another volunteer. "That's not out of the Bible!"

"I'm paraphrasing," retorted Emily, and they all laughed.

Whatever the theological truth, there was indeed not only buttered bread, but a platter of cold cuts, three different kinds of salad, two pies and a maple-walnut layer cake.

"Virtue rewarded," commented Mrs. McCurry as she refilled everyone's coffee mug.

Although all the volunteers were her mother's age or older, Coryn felt welcome and comfortable in this group. She knew they were all committed Christians and that a great deal of their life was centered in their church activities. She wondered how big a part this played in her mother's life. It was something they had never really discussed. Clare just quietly lived her faith in everything. It was so much a part of her.

Coryn felt a kind of emptiness inside, realizing that she had not developed more of those values her mother had tried to instill in her. She had neglected that part of her life during the last few years. No wonder she had made such poor choices, such wrong decisions, hadn't been able to tell the difference between the counterfeit and the real.

"All right, ladies, back to work. We've only got a few more baskets to go," Mrs. McCurry announced.

Shortly after they all returned to their posts, they heard dozens of feet scuffling along the corridor outside and children's voices. Soon, from an adjoining room, came the slightly off-key singing of Christmas carols.

"Hark, the herald angels sing!" quipped the irrepressible Emily.

"The junior choir rehearsing for the Christmas program," Dorothy, one of the other volunteers, explained to Coryn.

It did seem to add a special touch to their work hearing them. Finally all the baskets were filled, tagged, ready to go to another set of volunteers who would deliver them on Christmas Eve.

As Coryn got ready to leave, Mrs. McCurry said, "Thank you so much for coming to help us. It would have taken us much longer if you hadn't pitched in with your young energy and willing hands.''

"I really enjoyed it, Mrs. McCurry," Coryn told her, realizing she really had.

Outside, the wind was cold and Coryn hurried to her car. She was just unlocking her door, when she heard a horn tapped lightly. Turning, she saw Mark Emery sitting behind the wheel of his station wagon. He rolled down the window and called, "Hi!"

She turned and waved. "What are you doing here?''

"Waiting for Ginny. She's practicing for her big moment as an angel in the Christmas program."

"She won't have to practice very hard, she *is* one." Coryn smiled.

"Thanks. I could ask you the same question, I mean, what you're doing here?''

"Actually, filling in for my mother," she said. "Of course, we used to come here as a family." She paused. "I always wanted to be an angel in the Christmas program but they always picked the girls with long blond curls."

"They're more liberal about angels nowadays." Mark grinned.

"I certainly hope so." Coryn stood there for a minute. But there really wasn't anything more to say. "Well, I'm off. Merry Christmas," she said, and got in her car.

Mark watched her thinking he wished he'd said something more. Asked her for a date. *Date!* He hated that word. It seemed so juvenile somehow. But what else could he call it? He liked Coryn Dodge, he'd thought from the beginning she was someone he'd like to know. She was—well, a lot of things, and how else could he find out more unless he called her and asked her out?

Coryn waved to him again after she'd backed out and passed his car. Funny, running into him again. Here, of all places. And to find out Ginny attended Sunday school at the same church Coryn had as a child. And that she was in the Christmas pageant.

What a special guy Mark Emery must be. Obviously a great father. She remembered the reasons he'd told her for moving to Rockport. His values were certainly in the right place. Tragic about his wife. As she drove home, Coryn wondered what his wife had been like, Ginny's mother. It must be hard for Mark doing the things alone that ought to be shared.

From deep inside of Coryn came a longing for something, for someone to love, some fulfilling purpose to her life.

January

Chapter Nine

Christmas came. Coryn tried to enter into the spirit of it but it seemed to come and go before she could grasp the real meaning under all the glitter, the music, the presents. She had received invitations to parties to which she went, some given by her parents' friends and some by her contemporaries. She had a detached sense of not really belonging anymore. If she stayed in Rockport she would have to make more of an effort. But she wasn't sure yet if that's what she was going to do. She felt as if she was waiting for something. Direction?

Underneath it all she found herself wondering what kind of Christmas Mark and Ginny were having. Had Ginny received what she wanted from Santa? Were the Three Wise Men in place? Had it been a day of sad memories for Mark?

Preparations for her parents' New Year's Day party filled the week after Christmas. Her father had added several dozen people to the guest list. Names

Coryn couldn't place. When she asked her mother about them, she received a vague answer.

"They're mostly people he knows through Rotary and in business. I don't know some of them. He wanted them invited so—" She smiled. "He's testing the political waters, you know."

Coryn frowned. The idea that her father might run for the state assembly still seemed strange. He had a great personality for it—outgoing, gregarious, positive. But if elected, it would mean spending most of his time in Sacramento. She couldn't imagine her parents giving up their home, their friends, their pleasant life-style here in Rockport.

Well, it wasn't her decision to make. The week passed quickly and suddenly it was the day of the open house.

Coryn had a new dress—a rich blue velour with an empire waist, a scoop neck, long sleeves and a flowing ankle-length skirt—for which she had paid far too much. She had bought it thinking she would wear it to celebrate the new year with Jason. In the shop's dressing room she had known it was the most becoming dress she had ever owned. But now Jason would never see her in it. To her surprise, she realized she didn't care very much.

She brushed her freshly shampooed hair to a polished sheen, applied mascara and sprayed on perfume. She gave herself a final check in the mirror and went across the hall and tapped on her mother's bedroom door. To her surprise, Clare was still in her bathrobe, standing uncertainly in front of her open closet. She turned as Coryn came into the room. Her smile was brief, tentative, her eyes anxious. "It's the silliest thing, but I can't remember what I planned to wear."

"I thought you said you had a new dress."

"Oh, yes, *of course*. How stupid." Her mother laughed. "I'd forget my head if it wasn't attached. I suppose it's all the excitement of you coming home and all the fuss of getting ready for the holidays and this party that's rattled me."

Clare gave a nervous little laugh. "Did I tell you what happened downtown the other day when I was shopping? I went to write a check and couldn't find my checkbook. My credit cards and driver's license and everything. Imagine! I'd changed purses, taken it out and left it..." Her voice trailed off indecisively.

"Sounds like something I might do!" Coryn said quickly, but her stomach tightened. It was an uncharacteristic thing for her mother to have done. Her mother was organized about everything. Take her clothes closet. Everything arranged in perfect order by coordinating colors, shoes neatly stored in shoe trees, matching handbags on the shelves above in zippered plastic bags. It was her modeling training. Clare Dodge had been a model before her marriage. Her career had gotten off to a promising start, but she'd given it all up once she married Coryn's father simply because he'd asked her to.

Thrusting back a prickle of anxiety, Coryn said briskly, "Well, you better get ready, Mom. Dad will be pacing if you're not downstairs to greet guests with him."

Coryn stepped inside the walk-in closet and looked

around. She spotted a creamy silk dress, its draped bodice and long sleeves scattered with silver star-shaped sequins. She took it off the clothes rack and held it up. "Is this what you planned to wear?"

"Of course! How clever of you, darling."

Coryn had the awful feeling that unless *she* had found it, her mother would not *really* have known if this was the dress or not.

Clare put on her dress and Coryn zipped up the back. Then her mother seated herself at her dressing table to put on her makeup. Standing behind her, Coryn watched as graceful hands expertly dusted on blusher, applied mascara to her eyelashes. As her mother picked up her brush to give a final touch to her silver-blond hair, her eyes met Coryn's in the mirror. Almost as if her mother were waiting for her to say something, Coryn exclaimed, "You look beautiful, Mom."

A strangely pensive expression crossed Clare's face. A rather wistful smile lifted the corners of her mouth. "Beauty is in the eye of the beholder, don't they say? My stepfather didn't value beauty much. That's why he didn't feel they should spend the money to send me to college. 'She's got nothing going for her but her looks,' I overheard him tell my mother. You know, that devastated me." Clare shrugged. "Most teenage girls would have died for what I had then. But I wanted something more. I wasn't sure just what...but I believed eventually I would know." She sighed. "That's why I wanted to succeed at modeling, I guess. To show my stepfather. I guess I'm still trying to prove something to him."

Coryn didn't know how to respond. She had never heard about this incident before. So she said nothing. Her mother stood up, moved away from the mirror. She did a model's pirouette in the center of the floor then and cupped Coryn's chin lightly with cool fingers. "Thank you, darling, for your help. Come on, let's go downstairs and do your father proud. He's always happy to show off his wife and daughter."

Coryn was cheered by the lilt in her mother's voice. The sadness was gone from her eyes, the radiant smile was in place. Everything was all right again. Everything was fine. *Wasn't it?*

It was frightening to think anything was wrong with her mother. Her mother so confident, so charming, so with it. Ah, but there was something definitely missing now...something vital and important. Coryn just wasn't sure what.

As they went down the curving stairway together, Coryn thought of the memory her mother had just shared. Although it had happened years ago, it had shaped the direction of Clare's life. Her mother had never talked much about her childhood or her parents. Coryn had never known either of them, both had died before she was born.

In the front hall stood a glittering decorated Christmas tree. Gold and white angels, gilded pinecones, silvery bows and frosted bells hung from sweeping branches. Another example of her mother's artistry. Each of the rooms looked like a picture in one of those glossy-paged architectural magazines. The house smelled of cedar, cinnamon and some kind of spicy potpourri placed in porcelain bowls on tabletops and other surfaces in the spacious living room and dining room. The scent of burning apple logs crackling in the open fireplace mingled with scented candles alight on the mantelpiece and buffet table.

Door chimes began to ring with frequency. For the next hour, guests arrived, and flowed in chattering clusters through the festively decorated rooms.

Coryn dutifully circulated, stopping to speak to people who had not seen her for months, answered questions about her job, her life in L.A., smiling.

The buzz of conversation, the clink of glasses and sounds of laughter, merged around her. Groups of well-dressed people milled through the house, helping themselves to the plentiful food and drinks. The atmosphere was festive, but instead of making Coryn feel happy, she became increasingly anxious. It was ridiculous to feel depressed in the midst of all this gaiety, but she couldn't seem to help it. Then, as though she was expecting him, she turned toward the front door just as Mark Emery walked into the house.

Mark had sat in his car out in the driveway for a good ten minutes before getting out and going up to the house. He'd sat there asking himself why he had come to the Dodges' open house. The minute he had driven up the hill and seen the lights blazing out into the winter darkness, cars parked along the parkway and on either side of the street, he had almost turned around and gone home. From the number of cars, he realized it must be a big party. Judging from the make of the cars outside, he guessed that their owners, and the guests, must be some of Rockport's most affluent. His economy station wagon was hardly in the same league. Why hadn't he turned around and left? Because Coryn had asked him and because he wanted to see her again.

When he saw her, something happened. That same sense of recognition that he had felt in the S.F. Airport. Only then, they'd never met before. It was an uncanny sensation. It had been more than momentary attraction. What it might become, he didn't know.

As he walked into the house, he spotted her immediately, standing by the Christmas tree in the foyer. The lights sent sparkles glinting through her hair. When she saw him, her eyes lit up, too, and she smiled—almost as if she were waiting for him.

Suddenly there seemed to be no one else in the room, just the two of them.

Mark was a little stunned by his own reaction as Coryn moved gracefully toward him. He noticed she was wearing her hair differently tonight, swept up from her slender neck and back from her ears where blue pendant earrings swung. She looked altogether lovely.

"Hello, Mark, I'm glad you came," she said.

For a minute they'd just stood there smiling at each other. He was aware how blue her eyes were and of the perfume he remembered that seemed to move with her like a lovely cloud. Then Coryn's father came up and greeted him heartily. Coryn made the introductions.

"Good to meet you, Emery. My wife mentioned you might stop by. Come with me, there are some people you ought to meet," and he took Mark's arm and walked him away to introduce him to a group of guests.

Some time later Mark found his way back to Coryn. "Can we find someplace to talk? I came to see *you*."

"Dad has a way of taking over." She smiled.

"He'll make a good politician."

"You think so?"

"Has all the right stuff." Mark grinned.

Coryn led him to a windowed alcove in the living room and they sat down. "I guess that remains to be seen. I don't think he's decided. I'm not sure my mother is that for it."

"Politics is hard on families. I saw that when I worked at the *Sacramento Bee*. Sometimes a choice has to be made and the families get the short end."

"Families mean a great deal to you, don't they?"

"Yes. I think they *are* important. Growing up in a solid family is everything for a child."

"That's what you're doing for Ginny, isn't it?"

"Trying to."

"She's a sweet child. You must be doing it right," Coryn said then changed the subject. "Have you had something to eat, to drink?"

He shook his head.

"Let me get you something." She got up, saying, "I'll be right back."

All around him the party sounds swirled. Mark glanced around the room. This was a part of Rockport he'd only seen from a distance, as a reporter covering fancy fund-raising dinners and political events. He was sure the movers and shakers of the town were here tonight, with their expensively gowned wives. The Dodges belonged to this social scene. He didn't. Did Coryn? When they had dinner together in the airport restaurant, he had sensed, under her composure, a restlessness, a longing for something more. Her discontent with her job in L.A. had evidently resulted in her decision not to return. What would she do now? He knew he wanted to find out. To do that he'd have to get to know her better. Where that would lead was the question.

In a few minutes Coryn was back with a plate of sandwiches, deviled eggs, and balancing two cups of punch.

"So how does it feel being back in Rockport?" Mark asked.

"I don't think it seems real yet. I made the decision and I have to live with it but I'm not sure what comes next."

"The new year is always a good time for new beginnings, isn't it? Or at least it's supposed to be. Making resolutions and all that."

She made a small groan. "Making resolutions has never been my strong suit. It brings a lot of stuff to the surface. Old mistakes you don't want to repeat."

"New Year's resolutions can be sobering. I mean that in the most literal sense. I always think I'm going to make some. I rarely do." He paused, "I guess Rockport seems awfully provincial to you after L.A.?"

"No, I don't think that's my problem." She attempted a laugh. "If you could say I *have* a problem."

"Has it changed much?"

"I suppose. It's different. There's more going on now...culturally, I mean. The Civic Light Opera, Old Town, the Nautical Museum, the Repertory Theater..."

"Speaking of which—" Mark reached into his jacket pocket and held up two tickets. "The newspaper gets courtesy tickets. These are for their opening production of the year. Chekov's *Uncle Vanya.* Would you like to go?"

"Chekov? That's awfully ambitious for an amateur group, isn't it?"

"They're pretty good. I saw their last performance. Maybe you don't like Russian plays?"

"They do tend to be somewhat dark. All heavy drama, family secrets, hidden motives. Whatever happened to local theaters putting on *Charlie's Aunt* or *A Christmas Carol?*"

They both laughed.

"Ironic, isn't it that Dickens wrote so often about the ideal, happy family when his own home life was so terrible."

"Maybe everyone has his or her own fantasy of what constitutes a happy family," Coryn suggested.

"Tolstoy wrote, 'All families are unhappy in their own way.' In modern terms...all families are dysfunctional in their own style. What's dysfunctional to one person may seem normal to another, depending on the circumstances."

Coryn did not comment. Her idea of a happy family had always been her own. Now she wasn't so sure. It was like seeing a distorted image reflected in a mirror. That's how she'd felt since she came home. It had not shattered, thank God. But there was definitely a crack in the mirror.

Their conversation turned to lighter things yet Mark had the feeling that there was so much more they had to talk about. He had the strong sensation something was on the brink of happening between them. A man who knew Mark came up to discuss some current local event and claimed his attention. Coryn excused herself.

At length he felt he had stayed long enough, especially since he knew he and Coryn wouldn't have another chance to talk alone. He felt a little lift, thinking she looked somewhat disappointed when he told her he was leaving.

"Well, this has been very enjoyable but I better go. I told Mrs. Aguilar I'd be home by eight. In time to read Ginny her story and tuck her in." Mark grinned. "Start the new year right by being on time for work tomorrow morning."

"I'm glad you could come, Mark," Coryn said as she accompanied him into the hall. At the door she said, "Tell Ginny 'hi' for me."

"I'll do that. She's talked a lot about the day here with you and your mother, baking cookies and all." He halted a second then asked, "So, would you like to go with me next Thursday?"

"To the play?"

"Yes, *Uncle Vanya*."

"Yes, thank you. I'd like to, very much."

"Thursday night, then. I'll pick you up at seven-thirty. Curtain's at eight."

All the way home Mark thought about Coryn. He hadn't been sure about asking her out but when the conversation had turned to talk of plays, it just seemed natural to do so. Well, it wasn't a big deal. He'd found Coryn Dodge interesting, intelligent, a good conversationalist. And it would be interesting to see how a local group handled Chekov.

Okay, cut out the rationalization. Admit it. He was attracted to Coryn Dodge. No doubt about that. Furthermore, she was the first woman he'd felt that kind of attraction for since Shari. It wasn't as though he was falling in love or anything.

And yet, there was a kind of truth stirring. Unsettling. If this did develop into something serious, how would he feel? How would he handle it?

Was it too soon?

Soon? It had been three years. Three years was a long time to be alone. He knew his life was incomplete. He knew Ginny needed a mother. They both needed to be a family. But he didn't want to make a mistake. Loneliness wasn't sufficient reason to marry again.

He pulled into his driveway. Mrs. Aguilar had left the porch light on for him, otherwise the house was dark. He felt letdown somehow. It would be nice to have someone to come home to again.

Sighing heavily, he got out of the car. He better get to bed, he was due at the paper at seven-thirty.

Chapter Ten

Coryn had mentioned her theater date with Mark Emery to her parents. Casually. But inside she felt excited. With Mark she was on new ground. That he was such a contrast to Jason made it even better. It proved something. In fact, Jason was becoming more and more a thing of the past. A bad mistake she wanted to forget.

A recent phone conversation with Sheila had confirmed the wisdom of her decision not to go back to L.A., to break with him.

They had finished discussing the disposal of some of Coryn's belongings she didn't want shipped when Sheila said, "Oh, by the way, Jason phoned asking about some CDs of his that were missing from his collection. Wanted me to check if they were among ours, see if you'd taken them with you. Get that? What a nerve! I told him off but good. He didn't even ask about you, if you were coming back or what." Coryn felt the sting of humiliation but only said, "It doesn't matter, it was over between us even before I left."

"I never could understand what you saw in him. Shallow, arrogant jerk," Sheila retorted.

They talked a little longer before hanging up. Yet Jason's indifference hurt. Hadn't she meant anything to him? She had been so foolish. Echoing Sheila's question, what *had* she ever seen in Jason?

Thursday evening Coryn dressed with special care. She put on the new pink cashmere sweater her mother had given her for Christmas, and fastened in the pearl studs, her father's present. When she was ready a full half hour before he was due, she realized how much she was looking forward to being with Mark.

The play was labored, but the cast tried hard.

Mark and Coryn were swept into the vestibule of the theater with the flow of the departing audience. They stood for a minute near the box office.

"*Heavy,*" Mark said.

"*Very,*" she replied.

"I should have known what we were in for. Did it seem as long to you as that summer did to Uncle Vanya?"

Coryn laughed. They started walking across the street to where Mark had parked his car.

"Still," Coryn said, "I must say it was well done, for a nonprofessional cast."

"You're right. I guess you saw a lot of theater when you were in L.A."

"Actually not," Coryn replied, recalling that Jason liked to go to high-visibility restaurants or dinner clubs where he could see and be seen. By whom, she never really knew. Jason often table-hopped when he was with her, rarely introducing her to anyone. She had been so naive. Taking him at his own estimation. Simply glad to be with him. She had liked the feeling of other women's envious gazes following them. Who were these people he had tried so hard to impress? Probably only self-important climbers like himself.

"I'm glad I don't have to write the review," Mark said as he unlocked the passenger-side door and opened it for her to get in. He got in the driver's side. "I don't know why, but I am hungry. At least my stomach didn't fall asleep. How about you?"

"That sounds great."

"Al's?" he asked.

"Sure, why not?" They both laughed.

A sign boasted: Breakfast Served 24 Hours. Once in the red-vinyl booth Mark asked her, "What will you have—the Lumberjack, or the Woodsman's Special?"

"What's the difference?" She looked for a clue in the menu description.

"Lumberjack has hotcakes on the side, the Woodsman hash browns."

"The Woodsman then."

Their order given, the waitress left. For a minute they were quiet. Mark looked over at her. Coryn looked prettier than ever tonight. Pink was becoming to her, gave her skin delicacy and warmth. As if conscious of his regard, she lowered her eyes and her long lashes made tiny crescent shadows on her cheeks. She asked, "How is Ginny's eye?"

Mark grimaced. "It's an every morning hassle," he said in a low voice. "She doesn't like to wear the patch to school. Says the kids make fun of her. It always seems to disappear just as we're getting ready to leave." He shook his head. "I don't understand it. I'm sure Mrs. Aguilar puts it out in plain sight along with her clothes the night before. It's a mystery."

"Probably *The Borrowers*." Coryn smiled.

Mark frowned. "The Borrowers?"

She laughed. "It's a famous book series for children. I used to love it when I was Ginny's age. It explained all the things that disappear in a household. No one can ever find what happens. But the secret is there is a tiny family that lives behind the walls that take things—put them to their own use…"

Mark still looked puzzled.

"Oh, well, scratch that!" Coryn laughed. "It's probably not a 'guy thing'."

Their orders came, heaped plates smelling deliciously, were set in front of them. For a few minutes conversation slowed while they ate hearty food. Then they talked about all sorts of things.

Mark was easy to talk to. He was knowledgeable about what was current in books and films, politics. He was matter-of-fact, not arrogant, and clearly interested in hearing her opinion on various subjects. Coryn realized this was a different kind of date. She felt relaxed, instead of trying to make an impression, she was being herself. It was like talking to someone she had known for a long time, a friend. Coryn had never had a man friend. The idea intrigued her.

Over coffee Mark asked, "So, what is the real reason you decided not to go back to L.A.? When we were in San Francisco, I got the idea you felt you'd outgrown a small town like Rockport."

Coryn hesitated. Tell Mark the truth? Yes, she could trust him to fill in the blanks. He was perceptive enough.

"I was in a dead-end job and a dead-end relationship. I thought I'd give myself a new start."

"Sometimes the best thing you can do is just that. And don't look back. Clean slate." He paused, then said almost shyly, "I'm glad you decided to stay in Rockport."

Coryn felt inordinately pleased by the way he said it and by the way he was looking at her.

The waitress came with their check and to refill their coffee cups.

Mark told Coryn the subject of his next feature story, coastal lighthouses. "They're almost obsolete now, I mean, the romantic idea of the lone lighthouse keeper keeping the light burning for lost ships at sea, that sort of thing. But they've got a great history, one that shouldn't be forgotten. It means making some short trips to Mendocino and up the coast of Oregon. They're beautiful drives, and talking to some of the old-timers should be fascinating."

It was nearly one o'clock in the morning when they left the diner.

In the car, Mark turned on the car radio and as they drove along the winding roads to the Dodges' house in Chestnut Hills, they listened to a concert of semiclassical music with lots of strings.

Coryn felt a little tension start to creep over her. The other times she'd been with Mark they'd met by chance. This was their first real date. A *date* date.

The moment she always dreaded on "first dates" was fast approaching. Would he or wouldn't he? And should she or not?

When Mark turned in the driveway, the piece hadn't quite finished. They sat there listening until it ended. Coryn mentally held her breath.

The decision was made for her. Mark got out of the car, came around, opened the door on the passenger side for Coryn. They walked up to the front door and Coryn put her key in the lock. "Thanks, Mark, I enjoyed the evening."

"Next time we'll try for lighter entertainment," he said.

Coryn felt pleased. There would be a *next* time then. She pushed open the door and stepped inside the entryway. As she turned, he took her hand and drew her back. With one hand he brushed back her hair, then leaned toward her and kissed her.

Her hair was silky against his hand, her mouth was soft.

The kiss, light and very sweet, surprised her a little. Yet she returned it.

"Good night, Coryn," he said quietly. "I really enjoyed being with you. I'll call you soon."

"That would be great," Coryn replied realizing she meant it.

She stood there as he walked back to his car, got in, backed out of the driveway. She felt a little ripple of happiness. A feeling she almost didn't recognize. It had been so long since she had felt this way. And Mark's kiss. Had that really happened? Had she liked it as much as she thought she did?

Chapter Eleven

In the first weeks of the new year, Coryn often asked herself why had she never asked her mother about the Christmas presents in the trunk of her car? Coryn had gone along on another shopping trip with her mother, helping her pick out gifts for the same people whose presents were already wrapped, tagged. Was it just because she loved her mother, hadn't wanted to embarrass her? She had seen her cringe with humiliation when Coryn's father had brought up some lapse of memory or some omitted errand. Or was it because she was afraid? Afraid her mother hadn't remembered buying and wrapping them? Afraid there might be something seriously wrong with her mother?

With a tiny clutch of fear she thrust that thought away. It was probably only a temporary condition, maybe something to do with menopause. Coryn didn't want to accept the fact that her always youthful, vibrant mother was getting older.

Besides, Coryn's thoughts and time were more and more centered around Mark Emery. He had followed through on his promise to call. They had gone out several times after that. Mostly impromptu, casual dates. They'd met for lunch, gone to the movies and attended the opening of a new gallery in Old Town together. This appearance had occasioned introductions to some of Coryn's old friends. Cindy and her husband had also been there. Cindy had looked very curious when she saw who Coryn's escort was. She had phoned the next day for a report.

"So how long have you been seeing Mark Emery?" she asked. "I know a half-dozen people who have invited him to social events and he always turns them down. What's your secret?"

Coryn had laughed and tactfully dodged Cindy's probing.

"Just my charm and intelligence," she teased, then added, "We just have a lot in common."

"You do?" Cindy sounded doubtful. Then, "Well, if I decide to throw a dinner party or something will you bring him?"

"Sure, that is, if he'll come." Coryn agreed. "His work keeps him very busy and he has a little girl he spends a great deal of time with."

That seemed to satisfy Cindy for the moment. But after she put down the phone Coryn wondered if observers were already pegging them as a couple?

Besides these dates, on a couple of Sundays she had gone with Mark when he took Ginny to the park and the zoo. These times had been particularly enjoyable. Coryn had never been around children very much but she found Ginny a very sweet and endearing child.

Coryn realized that in a very short while she was spending substantial time with them and thinking about them. Mark's remark about Ginny's reluctance to wear her eye patch had stayed with Coryn. How to get her to do what was necessary and yet make it fun was the problem. Could she figure out a way to help them both? To make wearing the patch a happy experience and somehow make Ginny feel special?

Coryn wasn't exactly sure when she got the idea but once she did, she wasted no time starting the project. Why not make covers that would slip over the leather patch, pretty ones, colorful, fanciful to match some of Ginny's outfits?

Coryn went to the fabric store and bought squares of different colored fabric and felt, assorted ribbons and trim. At home, she cut out two for samples; one she made like a sunflower with brown center and bright yellow petals, the other she made a clown face.

When she finished them she had a few second thoughts. Would Ginny like them or think them silly? Would Mark think she was being too pushy, insinuating herself, her ideas into a private family matter. Well, the only thing to do was to find out.

Taking the two patches, she drove over to Mark's house. She'd never been there. She looked up the address and ventured over one weekday morning. She thought Mrs. Aguilar, the housekeeper, would be the best one to approach first. She was curious to meet this paragon, whose praises both Mark and Ginny sang unreservedly.

Mark's house was a sloping-roofed, brown shingle, the style known as California bungalow popular in the 1920s. There was a front porch and a huge holly tree, red with berries, on one side of the flagstone path leading up to the house.

She heard the old-fashioned doorbell echo inside the house and a few minutes later the door was opened by a plump, middle-aged woman, in a flowered apron. Her salt and pepper hair was braided in a coronet above a round face with very dark, shiny brown eyes.

"Yes?" she said as if Coryn might be selling something.

"Hi, I'm Coryn Dodge, a friend of Mark's. And Ginny's, too, of course. And you must be Mrs. Aguilar."

Did Mrs. Aguilar's expression change from caution to suspicion? Coryn wasn't sure but plunged on. This was a potential adversary that must be won. Without analyzing it, she realized she wanted the housekeeper to like her. It suddenly seemed important that she did.

"Mark told me he was having some trouble getting Ginny to wear her eye patch and I know it's really necessary that she does. So, I—" Coryn was watching Mrs. Aguilar closely as she pulled the two patch covers out of the bag she was carrying and held them up "—so I thought putting these on top might help."

A smile broke on Mrs. Aguilar's face.

"Why, if that isn't the cleverest thing! Well, if anything will help get the child to wear her patch these will. How kind of you to go to all that trouble." Mrs. Aguilar's voice was genuinely pleased and the sharp eyes had softened.

"I'm so glad you think so. I wanted to get your opinion. That's why I brought them by now when I knew Mark would be at work and Ginny at school. I thought you'd know best if this would work."

"I don't see why it wouldn't! My, aren't they pretty?"

Coryn hesitated, then thought she'd come this far why not? She took a deep breath. "I wondered if she had a favorite dress or an outfit that I could make a special one for her to wear with it?"

"Of course! Won't you come in and I'll show you Ginny's things. I've just been ironing and have some of them handy."

She opened the door wider for Coryn to come inside and led her through the hall to a utility room behind the kitchen, where an ironing board was set up in front of a small portable TV set on the counter.

Mrs. Aguilar clicked it off and one by one held up a red and green plaid dress with ruffled collar, a bright blue jumper and striped blouse. "And then her red parka she wears every day. Maybe you could make one for that." The housekeeper was really entering into the project enthusiastically.

Coryn jotted some quick notes in the small notebook she kept in her handbag.

"This is awfully kind of you, Miss Dodge," Mrs. Aguilar said. "To take such an interest—" her voice trailed off. She looked directly at Coryn, an unspoken question in her eyes. Coryn suddenly felt self-conscious and glanced away. Then Mrs. Aguilar continued, "I worry about both of them. I do what I can but there's something missing in a house when there's no mother," Mrs. Aguilar said with concern then her manner turned cheerful again. "Won't you stay and have a cup of coffee or tea with me?"

Coryn felt she had passed some invisible test and smiled.

"Why, yes, thank you, that would be lovely."

Mrs. Aguilar busied herself with the kettle and getting out cups and saucers. She arranged some gingersnap cookies on a plate and set it on the table. Coryn had the feeling that the housekeeper was considering saying more. The tea brewed, the housekeeper brought the china teapot to the table, then sat down across from Coryn and held out the plate to offer her a cookie.

"As I say, I do my best," she said as she filled Coryn's cup with the steaming fragrant tea. "And Mr. Emery is certainly a fine man. A child couldn't ask for a better father. But nothing makes up for losing your mother. Especially for a girl, I think."

The housekeeper was definitely giving Coryn an opening. But Coryn felt too shy to take it. All she could manage was to say, "I'm awfully fond of both Mark and Ginny."

"I'm glad. Ginny's talked about you often." Mrs.

Aguilar seemed satisfied. They chatted for another fifteen minutes or so then Coryn left, leaving the eye patch covers for Ginny. It was such a simple gesture, actually, yet as she drove away from the small, brown-shingled house, Coryn felt inextricably bound to it and its occupants. It was a sense of belonging that she had never quite experienced before. It had all sorts of happy possibilities.

That night Ginny, in pyjamas, robe and furry slippers, brought the tattered copy of her favorite book into the living room for Mark to read to her. Smelling sweetly of shampoo and talcum, she cuddled up in the crook of Mark's arm beside him in his armchair. "Now read," she directed, and he opened *The Velveteen Rabbit.*

He had read it a dozen times before, over and over, because it was usually Ginny's request. Sometimes he persuaded her to choose an alternate one but it was to this story that they returned the most often. Why, then, tonight, did the words he had spoken so many times in the past seem to ring true in his ears, as if he were hearing it for the first time? They seemed to have special meaning, as though they had been written especially for him to hear, to absorb.

Mark tucked Ginny in, kissed her good-night, received several hard hugs in return, turned on the night-light and walked back into the living room. The book, with its worn edges, faded cover of the floppy-eared rabbit, was beside his chair. He picked it up and held it, looking at it thoughtfully. Love is what

makes a person real. Genuine, authentic, truthful—
vulnerable. As if he heard it spoken, this came
through to him very clearly. Unless you allow yourself to be real, you'll never know love again.

Love requires sharing yourself with another person. Sharing your true feelings takes courage. Risk.
Faith.

He remembered Shari once teasing him, saying,
"If anything should happen to me, if I should die
first, you better get married again quick. Otherwise
you'll start getting too many picky bachelor habits—
Mr. Neatnik."

He picked up one of the eye patch covers Coryn
Dodge had made for Ginny, fingered it thoughtfully.
She had acted spontaneously, out of compassion for
a little girl's embarrassment about looking different
and turned it into something that made her feel special. She had done it out of kindness and affection
and caring. He felt touched and warmed by it. Ginny
had been so happy. It was something he would never
have thought to do. Even Mrs. Aguilar was impressed. Why would Coryn have bothered if she
didn't feel something *real* for them? For him as well
as Ginny. What was he so afraid of? Of being *real?*
Of being *hurt?* What was it the book said, loving
you run the risk of being hurt? But he wouldn't have
missed loving Shari even knowing what had happened, even knowing the hurt that would be his after
her accident. No one could have predicted that. If he
and Coryn went on—if something *real* developed be-

tween them— So be it! Mark decided he was willing to risk it.

A few days later in her mail, Coryn received a laboriously printed note from Ginny extravagantly decorated with crayoned daisies, colorful stickers and an arched rainbow.

DEAR CORYN,
THANK YOU FOR THE PRETTY PATCHES.
THEY MADE ME HAPPY.
                                    LOVE GINNY

The next week, after watching a foreign film at the University theater Coryn invited Mark in for coffee and homemade brownies. In the kitchen, Coryn let Ranger in from the utility room and he and Mark made friends. Mark sat on his heels stroking the Lab's head and looked up at Coryn as she measured out coffee. "Great dog."

"Yes. He's been my pal since sixth grade."

"Children and pets, go together. As I've been told!" he laughed. "Ginny wants one but I don't want to put another burden on Mrs. Aguilar. She has enough to do just looking after us."

Ranger took his place under the kitchen table when Coryn brought their cups and a plate of brownies.

Mark took one and bit into it, holding up his hand with his thumb and forefinger making a circle, indicating it was delicious.

"You know there's something familiar about all this," he said, then asked, "Did I ever tell you about the uncanny feeling I had when I first saw you in the San Francisco Airport—that I might have met you?"

Coryn shook her head.

"Well it was just a quick flash. Then I knew, of course, I hadn't," he paused, smiling. "I would have remembered." He went on, "But now it just seems so natural—I mean, like we've known each other for a long time, been friends."

"I feel that way, too. Not that first meeting, but now."

Mark looked around with satisfaction. "Kitchens are cozy places. The heart of a home. I think they say a lot about the people who live there, don't you?"

"I guess so, I just never thought about it."

"I remember my grandmother's kitchen. I loved going there when I was a kid. There was always this wonderful smell, something cooking or baking. It gave me a good, secure feeling."

"Where did you grow up, Mark? I don't think you ever said."

"A small mid-west town, in Ohio, a place you never heard of. I had the typical Norman Rockwell boyhood, little league, Scouts, swimming at the lake, going fishing with my dad—Sounds corny, huh?"

"No, it sounds wonderful!" Coryn said. "Ideal. The kind of childhood everyone wishes they had, the kind everyone wants for their own children."

Mark reached across the table and took Coryn's hand.

"You, too, Coryn? You would opt for the vine-covered cottage with the white picket fence?" His tone was half teasing, half serious.

"Of course! In a heartbeat!" As soon as the words were out of her mouth Coryn's cheeks got warm.

"I would have thought that maybe you wanted something more sophisticated—" He squeezed her hand, "I'm glad I was wrong."

Mark started to ask, *How about kids? Do they go with the picture? Even someone else's kid?* But he thought he might be pushing his luck. Or worse still, leading to subjects he wasn't quite ready to discuss and letting Coryn know just how serious he was beginning to feel about her, about them.

Any further discussion was sharply interrupted when Ranger, a husky growl deep in his throat, scrambled to his feet, his nails scratching on the vinyl floor, he skidded to the back door and began to bark.

Coryn rolled her eyes and got up, saying to Mark, "Chipmunks in the backyard. They drive him crazy. He used to have great fun chasing them away. Now all he can do is bark."

She gently tugged Ranger back by his collar, talking soothingly to him and patting him at the same time.

Mark rose. "I've got to be on my way." He leaned down to pat Ranger's head. "Too bad, ol' fella, but my car will probably do the job for you when I turn on the headlights."

As Coryn walked through the house to the front door with him, he held her hand. In the hall, their goodnight kiss was longer than usual.

Chapter Twelve

It was one of those rare days that happen sometimes on the north coast in winter, a cloudless blue sky, bright sun, brisk wind. In the morning, Mark called.

"School's closed, county teachers' meeting. I'm playing hooky from the paper and taking Ginny to the beach. Want to come along?"

Without a moment's hesitation, Coryn said, "Yes."

"Good. How soon can you be ready?"

"Half an hour?"

"Great. We'll pick you up then." He rang off.

Coryn put down the phone, scrambled to change into a warm sweater, flannel-lined jeans. Even on a sunny day, north-coast beaches could be cold. When she came downstairs, she glanced out to look for Mark's station wagon then went into the kitchen to tell her mother where she was going.

"With Mark and Ginny? That will be fun. What

a nice man and what a precious child. Would you like to take along something to drink, some snacks?''

"Good idea." Coryn kissed her mother's cheek. Coryn felt happy, Clare seemed so well, her old self, it was a glorious day and she was looking forward to spending it with Mark and Ginny. She helped pack a bag with snacks and small cans of juice.

"You and Mark will want coffee," her mother said, pouring steaming coffee into a thermos jug. Mark and Ginny arrived a few minutes later.

With an eye patch, and wearing a red knit cap with its dangling yarn pompom, Ginny looked like a rakish little elf.

They parked the station wagon on the bluff overlooking the beach and walked down the dunes to the beach. The salt-tinged wind was sharp. The sun and fine weather had brought others out, as well. One couple had two frisky little dogs who were yipping and running into the surf. As Ginny stood watching them, the woman handed her a small stick and told her to throw it to see if one of the dogs would fetch it. Ginny was into the game in a flash. The little dogs loved it, and they continued as long as Ginny would toss it.

Coryn and Mark followed, laughing and cheering Ginny on as the two small dogs played tirelessly. Coryn vividly remembered bringing Ranger out here. He would race, wheel, leap barking into the waves, chase the seagulls then come back. She'd toss a stick over and over. He'd run down the beach after it, head held high, come prancing back triumphantly to drop it at her feet.

"This is *so* fun!" exclaimed Ginny, running back to them, catching both their hands and swinging them. "Isn't it, Daddy?"

"You bet. Great fun."

Mark's laughing eyes met Coryn's over Ginny's head. Coryn felt a surge of happiness. The sense of freedom to *be* happy that she had somehow lost.

One of the little dogs came scampering up to Ginny with the stick in his mouth, circling and crouching, as if saying, "Come play some more!" Ginny dropped both their hands and was off again in another round of tossing and fetching.

As Ginny ran in front of them down the beach, Mark caught Coryn's hand in his. Her heart gave a small flip as his fingers closed around her hand, their palms touching. She glanced at him. He was looking at her. Her breath became shallow.

He stopped, turned her into his arms in a hug, then kissed her.

When the kiss ended, Coryn stepped back and they smiled at each other. Her arms slowly slid from his shoulders and moved down to clasp his, still holding her around the waist. For a few seconds they looked into each other's eyes. Then they started walking down the beach again together.

The morning sped by. Ginny made friends with two little girls, sisters, whose parents had brought them. She shared the graham crackers from the bag Coryn's mother had fixed, and the three of them had a great time building a sand fort. Mark and Coryn sat nearby on a weathered log watching them and talking. They seemed to have lots to say to each other, never running out of topics.

The sun moved high in the sky. Their watches told them it was past noon. They called to Ginny and climbed back up the dunes, clambered up on the stone jetty. The wind at their backs, they walked toward the Seascape, an old lighthouse converted into a restaurant.

The place was warm and crowded, filled with the sound of voices and laughter, the clatter of dishes. Fishermen sat up along the counter, swapping stories of weather and tall tales about the size and quantity of their day's catch. Savory smells emanated from the kitchen area, the swinging door constantly opening and closing. Waitresses brought out loaded trays, busily serving orders while flirting with and making snappy replies to the teasing patrons, most of whom seemed to be as comfortable here as in their own homes.

Mark and Coryn found a table with an ocean view. The surf was rough and high, dashing against the rocks.

A waitress with flaming henna hair and dangling earrings made of shells brought them each a glass of water, then poured two mugs of fresh coffee and placed them before Mark and Coryn, asking cheerfully, "What'll it be, folks?"

Coryn and Mark ordered chowder, a famous specialty of Seascape. Ginny chose fish and chips.

"Today was fun, wasn't it?" Ginny asked, lifting her glass of water carefully and taking a sip.

"It sure was," Coryn agreed.

"The dogs were really fun," Ginny said. "I liked throwing the sticks for them and saying fetch like their owner told me to."

She put down her glass and looked directly at Coryn. "Did you have a pet when you were a little girl, Coryn?"

"Uh-oh, here we go," Mark said in a resigned voice.

"Did you?" Ginny persisted.

"Yes, a dog, Ranger. I still have him. He's getting pretty old now. He has arthritis."

"How old?"

"For a dog, very old."

"Did you take care of him yourself?"

"Well, sometimes I forgot, then…" Coryn started to say *my mother* did it for me. She darted a quick look at Mark but he was buttering his French bread and didn't meet her gaze. He was leaving her this round.

"*I* wouldn't forget," Ginny said. "Not if I had a little kitten."

The waitress returned with bowls of creamy clam chowder. As she set down Ginny's platter of fish sticks and French fries, she asked playfully, "Think you can manage all that, young lady?"

"Yes, thank you," Ginny said politely.

What a really lovely child she was, Coryn thought with a rush of tenderness as she watched her eat. Ginny's fingers, the little one curved daintily, dipped each of the fries into the small cup of catsup at the edge of her plate, taking small bites, then wiping her mouth with her napkin. Someone had taught her manners, all right. It amused Coryn that once they had been served, Ginny picked up the subject of pets again as if there had been no interruption.

"A kitty wouldn't be all that much trouble, would it, Coryn?" She glanced at Mark. "I promise, Daddy, I'd do everything myself. You wouldn't have to remind me."

"Even the litter box?" Mark asked.

Ginny had just taken a bite of French fry so only nodded. When she finished chewing, she said to Coryn, "I already have a name for one. Sunny. Isn't that a nice name for an orange kitty?"

Mark moaned. "I give up! Subtlety, thy name is *not* woman!" He laughed.

"Ready for dessert, folks?" Their waitress was back. "Homemade apple pie with cinnamon sauce or á la mode?" she asked, giving her pencil a little twirl.

Coryn looked doubtful. "I'm pretty full but... maybe, could we share one, Ginny?"

The little girl grinned. "Yes, please."

"Ice cream or sauce?"

"What shall it be, Ginny?" asked Coryn.

"*You* choose."

"Ice cream."

"I would have choosed that, too." Ginny grinned happily.

They drove home singing several rollicking renditions of the sea chanty "Blow the Man Down." They sung it over and over until Mark pleaded a change of tune. With lots of laughter and a couple of false starts, Ginny and Coryn sang some songs

Ginny had learned at Brownies that Coryn remembered from her own Girl Scout days. Coryn felt a warm happiness spread all through her. It seemed as if the three of them had always been together. As though they were meant to be.

As they passed the Rockport city-limit sign, Mark asked, "Mind if I make a quick stop at the grocery store. It's Mrs. Aguilar's day off. My night to be chef."

Coryn pretended disbelief. She looked at Mark with mock astonishment. "Is cooking one of your hidden talents?"

"Daddy's a good cook," piped up Ginny. "Yummy hamburgers and French fries...mmm." She rolled her one visible eye.

"Obviously you have a fan," Coryn said to Mark.

"My cheering section. I think she likes the dessert on these nights best. Sara Lee to the rescue." He grinned.

"'Scuse me, Coryn," Ginny said, leaning over the back seat. "I have to ask Daddy something and I need to whisper."

"Is that really necessary, honey? Whispering is rude, remember?"

"I know but..."

"It's okay with me, Ginny. I won't listen," Coryn said.

In a stage whisper that was hard not to overhear, Ginny asked Mark, "Can Coryn have supper with us?"

"I don't know whether she'd like to...but sure, of course," Mark told Ginny. To Coryn, he said,

"Would you? Willing to take a chance?" He looked at her questioningly.

"Please, Coryn." Ginny tilted her head to one side. "We don't get to have company very often."

"Well, then, I'll be your company. Thank you very much."

"Goody!" Ginny clapped her hands.

"Drop me off at my house first. I'll get rid of some of the sand and stuff. I'll drive over later. What time?"

"About six. If that's not too early. Ginny has school tomorrow and I have to be at the paper at seven-thirty, so we have early evenings."

"That's fine. I'll be there."

As Coryn got out of the car, Ginny giggled and called after her the old joke Mark had taught her on the way home. "See you later, alligator!"

"In a while, crocodile!" Coryn called back, laughing.

Chapter Thirteen

Arriving at the Emerys' house, she rang the doorbell, then heard voices and running footsteps. The door opened and Ginny stood, shyly smiling.

Mark was not far behind.

"Hi, come in. We're getting things lined up. Mrs. Aguilar left us all sorts of instructions."

"She *always* does on Daddy's night in the kitchen!" chirped Ginny, then clapped her hand to her mouth, "Whoops, sorry!"

"Rumors." Mark grinned. "Here, let me take your jacket."

Coryn had changed into a plum colored tunic sweater and matching pants. She had tied her hair back with a velvet ribbon and wore silver and turquoise earrings. Mark's gaze moved over her appreciatively.

The first time Coryn had been here, the day she had come bringing Ginny's eye patch covers, Mrs. Aguilar had taken her right to the back of the house.

Later, they had sat in the kitchen. She had not really seen the rest of the house.

From the center hall, Coryn saw two rooms. One was the living room, the other, from the glimpse she got through half-open glass doors, had probably originally been the dining room. It looked as though it had been turned into an office with a desk, computer and bookcases. It probably served as his study when Mark worked at home, she realized.

"Come in. I got a fire going, should take the chill off," Mark said. "Would you like something to drink? Soda, coffee? I've some apple cider simmering."

"That sounds good."

Mark rubbed his hands together. He seemed a little nervous. Ginny had told her that they didn't have company often. Did that include Mark entertaining ladies?

"Fine. Make yourself comfortable. Ginny, you want to help me?"

Ginny trotted off to the back of the house alongside him.

Coryn walked over to the fireplace, held out her hands to its glowing warmth, turned back, studied Mark's home.

On one side of the fireplace was a worn leather armchair and reading lamp. In front was a sofa, beside it a smaller armchair with matching, rather faded chintz covers. On both sides of the hearth were built-in bookcases crammed with books. There were lots of children's books on the lower shelves, easily accessible for Ginny.

Mark's domain was in sharp contrast to Jason's condo. Coryn remembered the first time she saw Jason's apartment. The address was a good one with an expensive view. The huge living room had glass doors leading out to a balcony overlooking the pool. Modern prints hung on the stark white walls. Furniture consisted of a contoured white sofa and a black-leather Eames chair. In front of the couch was a coffee table with a free-form glass top on which were neatly piled copies of *GQ* and *Fortune*. There was a gleaming black entertainment center with a twenty-four-inch television and CD cabinet. An exercise machine stood in one corner.

In Jason's black-and-white tile kitchen, the size of a boat galley, there was a chrome microwave and an automatic coffeemaker. It had struck her at the time that although he had lived there two years, the place looked like a high-priced motel room. As though Jason was just passing through, on the way to somewhere, on the way up. As it turned out, on the way out, out of her life.

The rattle of cups and spoons on a tray signaled Ginny's return. Holding the tray with both hands, Ginny approached with careful steps. Mark followed with a steaming server of apple cider.

Ginny put the tray down on the low coffee table, then stepped back, looked at Mark.

"That smells delicious," Coryn said.

"There are cinnamon sticks in each mug," Ginny told her, pointing. "You stir them and they kind of melt into the cider. It tastes yummy."

After they finished the cider, Ginny asked, "Would you like to see my room, Coryn?"

Over Ginny's head Coryn met Mark's gaze. He gave an imperceptible nod and smiled.

"While you ladies take an inspection tour, I'll get the charcoal started."

Ginny was small and wiry. She had lost her baby fat and would soon be all arms and skinny legs. Her hair was short, cut with bangs. If it had a tendency to curl, Coryn couldn't tell. Perhaps this style had been decided upon because it was quick and easy, needed no dexterity for French braiding or some other kind of hairstyle a little girl might like.

"Mrs. Aguilar made the curtains," Ginny said, skipping over to the high windows. "They match the dust ruffle on my bed, see?"

Coryn admired them, then Ginny pointed out her small old-fashioned school desk. "We found it in a junk shop. Well, not really junk, sort of an antique shop." She put her head to one side and grinned impishly. "Daddy hates them but Mrs. Aguilar says, 'You just never know what you might find there.' And we found this."

There was a low bookshelf with books and games and a floor lamp beside a small rocking chair. Then Coryn saw the dollhouse. It was empty. No furniture, no little doll occupants.

"Is this new? Something you're working on?" she asked.

Ginny shook her head. "It's a kit. My gramma sent it for Daddy to put together. We were going to finish it—but we sort of…'' She gave a little shrug. ''A dollhouse family needs a daddy *and* a mommy.''

It wasn't said sadly, just matter-of-factly. But the little girl's words made Coryn wince.

She thought of the elaborate dollhouse she had received the Christmas she was ten. Now she realized what a project it must have been for her parents. Especially her mother. The hours that had gone into the furnishing, the wallpaper, tiny curtains, coverlets for the beds. She also remembered the wonderful small china family that had come to live there, with a lace-capped grandmother and tweed-coated grandpa, even a small framed sampler cross-stitched ''Home Sweet Home'' that hung in the parlor.

Every little girl should have a dollhouse family. Coryn would have to ask Mark if she could give hers to Ginny.

''I guess we better go back. Daddy'll be wondering what's keeping us,'' Ginny said.

The evening passed with incredible speed and it was Ginny's bedtime before anyone realized. With one minor protest met with Mark's firm, ''School tomorrow, honey, I'll be up in a few minutes, to hear your prayers and tuck you in.''

Ginny made a reluctant start then asked, ''You'll come again, won't you, Coryn?''

''Thank you, Ginny, I'd love to.''

''We want her to, don't we, Daddy?'' Ginny glanced at Mark.

''Sure thing,'' Mark answered. Ginny lingered a moment longer until Mark said with a grin, ''Quit stalling, young lady.''

"I'm not, Daddy, I just—" she hesitated. "Is it okay if I give Coryn a hug?"

"Of course you can!" Coryn said feeling a rush of pleasure, and holding out her arms. Ginny ran across the room and into them. Her body felt small and warm and incredibly dear against Coryn as she held her for a minute.

Ginny wiggled loose then said, "'Night, Coryn."

"'Night, honey," Coryn replied, her voice suddenly husky.

"Now, scoot," Mark said and with a mischievous grin Ginny skipped out of the room calling over her shoulder, "I'll call you when I'm ready, Daddy."

The two adults looked at each other and laughed softly. "She's a darling, Mark. You've done a great job bringing her up."

A shadow passed over his face before he answered.

"I've tried. It's a big job. Mrs. Aguilar has been a tremendous help. I couldn't have done it without her."

Ginny's piping little voice called, "I'm ready, Daddy."

"Okay, hon. Coming." Mark unfolded himself from the deep chair. "Will you excuse me, Coryn? This may take a while. I don't like rushing bedtime. It's important to make a child feel safe, secure at nighttime."

"Of course," Coryn answered, thinking what a good father Mark was, patient, sensitive, understanding. She could see how hard he tried to make up for the loss of Ginny's mother.

After Mark left, Coryn got up. She wanted a closer look at some of the photographs she'd seen along the top bookshelf. There were lots of them. Pictures that could be captioned Happy Family.

Coryn picked up one of a gamine-faced young woman with wide dark eyes, a smiling mouth, short dark hair. Shari. There were pictures of her with Mark on a tennis court, each holding rackets, some photos of them sitting in beach chairs, palm trees in the background. Mexico? Hawaii? Honeymoon? Then Ginny began to appear in the shots, as a baby, a toddler. The photographs all seemed to stop when Ginny was about three.

On the lower shelf there was a picture of Shari against a snowy background, in ski togs, dark glasses pushed up on her head, smiling. Was that the weekend it had happened? The terrible accident Mark had told her about. Knowing the story, it broke Coryn's heart to look at the pictures. Why did Mark keep them on display? Coryn decided he probably wanted to keep Shari fresh in Ginny's memory, remind her that she had had a loving mother, that they had been a family.

When Mark came back after putting Ginny to bed, she asked, "All settled?"

"Yes. The last drink of water, the last hug, all settled." He grinned and sat down on the sofa beside her.

"She's a treasure, Mark."

"Yep, a great kid." He nodded. "By the way, I've made a decision. And you're responsible."

Coryn looked surprised. "Me? How?"

"I've decided to let Ginny have a pet. A kitten is what she wants."

"I really think it will be good for her, Mark."

"Will you go with us, help us pick one out?"

"Sure. I'd love to. The animal shelter always has dozens of kittens available. They have their shots and everything. They're ready to take home."

"If I regret this, I'll know who to blame," he teased. "Ginny's not above using you to nag me, you know. 'Coryn had a dog when she was a little girl.'" Mark imitated Ginny's childish tone.

Coryn laughed. "I don't think you'll regret it, Mark. Making a child happy has to be the best possible thing to do."

"Yes, that's true," he agreed.

"You've done a great job, Mark. Ginny's a wonderful little girl," Coryn added.

"Thanks. She had a good start. Shari was a superb mother. I also have to give Mrs. Aguilar lots of credit. Ginny's like one of her own grandchildren to her."

"Don't sell yourself short, Mark. Girls have a special relationship with their fathers. I know. And Ginny absolutely adores you."

Mark put another log on the fire, then came to sit beside Coryn on the sofa. He didn't say anything for a minute, then sighed and said, "It still doesn't make up for not having a mother."

"Of course not, but—" Coryn started to suggest that maybe some day there would be someone else, not to take Shari's place, but to make up for that loss by creating another place in Ginny's life, an important but different place. But she stopped herself from saying that. It would seem too intrusive, too self-asserting. Besides, she asked herself, would I be ready to take all this on even if Mark was thinking of *me?*

Another silence fell between them. The flames of the new log flared brightly and the wood crackled as it burned. There was a certain intimacy simply sitting together in the firelight. Coryn was very conscious of Mark's nearness. A kind of inner tremor shot through her, an inner knowing. Mark was a man she could trust, someone she could fall in love with. That sudden conviction made her nervous and she shifted her position, moving a little away from him. At almost the same time, his arm went around her shoulder. Then he kissed her. There had been no anticipation that it would happen and yet no hesitation. It seemed as natural as breathing. It was a good kiss, a satisfying kiss without being demanding. A kiss that held a promise she found exciting.

Suddenly the bell chime of the marine clock in the hallway struck ten. Was it sounding a warning for her heart? She sat up, moving out of the circle of Mark's arm, "Time for me to go."

As he helped her on with her coat, she said, "It's been a wonderful day, Mark."

"There'll be others I hope, Coryn," he said in a low voice.

He turned her around and drew her close and kissed her again. The kiss was slow, very sweet. When it ended, she stepped back and they looked at each other smiling. As if acknowledging there would be other kisses just as there would be other times.

He walked her out to her car, opened the door so she could slide in the driver's seat.

Although she had not planned to, she put her arm around his neck, drew his head forward and very deliberately kissed him on the mouth. "Today was very special, Mark."

Driving home through the dark streets Coryn felt happy. It had been such a fantastic evening, so right, so natural to be with Mark and Ginny. As if somehow it was something they'd done before and might go on doing.

Cooking supper together had been fun. Ginny had made the hamburger patties, shaping the meat into flat circles with little hands, for Mark to grill. They all had made the salad, laughing as they took turns adding cut up carrots, celery, bits of broccoli to the bowl of torn lettuce, making jokes about a "tossed salad." It was a joy to hear Ginny laugh, to see the tender amusement in Mark's eyes observing her.

It had felt so cozy, like a family. Maybe that was dangerous thinking. After her experiences of dating in L.A. Coryn had almost given up on the idea that men of character and commitment were still around. A man like Mark Emery would be easy to fall in love with. What she wasn't ready for was to be hurt again. But then love sometimes just happened.

At the memory of Mark's kiss Coryn smiled as she turned into the driveway. Ready or not, maybe she had already fallen in love with Mark Emery.

* * *

Mark stood on the sidewalk watching Coryn's car make a boulevard stop, the taillight blinking as she made the turn, then he walked slowly back into the house.

He made himself a cup of coffee and brought it into the living room. He felt somewhat uneasy.

Today had been really wonderful. He'd felt happier than he had for a long time. Although he was undeniably attracted to Coryn Dodge, he wondered if getting seriously involved with anyone was the right thing to do. Sometimes he thought it would be best if he didn't get into a serious relationship with anyone until Ginny was older. Grown up even. Ginny had lost her mother and sometimes seeing her longing for that special presence in her life made his heart ache. But other times he thought it was best if some other woman didn't try to fill that empty place.

Yet he felt a deep-seated loneliness. The need, the longing, to share his life with someone was strong. But was Coryn Dodge the one? Was he getting in too deep, too fast with Coryn? He didn't want to make a mistake. It was too important a step. Maybe, he'd better slow down, be cautious.

Chapter Fourteen

A week went by, then two. Mark hadn't called. Coryn was wracked with all kinds of doubts.

Why hadn't he called? Was he on assignment, out of town? Maybe Ginny was sick. Some childhood illness, like chicken pox or mumps? Still, he would have called, wouldn't he? He must have seen how fond she'd become of his little girl. She would have sent her a funny get-well card or a book or a game she could play in bed.

As each day passed, Coryn had to wonder if she'd handled things wrong again. With Mark, as she had with Jason. Come on too strong, seemed too eager? But with Mark, everything had felt so natural. So relaxed. So right. There'd been a spontaneous camaraderie, shared interests.

There was definite physical attraction, as well. She was sure of that. His kiss the evening they'd gone to the play, the kiss on the beach, the kiss that evening they'd spent together at his house. *That* had not been a *casual* kiss. It had awareness, excitement and passion. Passion held in check, but nevertheless, it had been there. What's more, Mark couldn't have mistaken *her* response to the kiss. Had she opened herself up too soon? Maybe that was it.

She'd thought a lot about relationships since Jason. She'd decided that Jason's rules of no strings, no commitment was shallow and wrong. Integrity, generosity, accountability was what she was looking for, what she wanted to give. Mark had too much character to play games.

By the end of the second week she hadn't heard from him, Coryn gave up making excuses. There could be any number of reasons. She wasn't going to allow herself to brood. She hated that she had regressed to listening for the phone, hoping Mark would call. Nonetheless, one afternoon when the phone rang she jumped to answer it.

"Hello." She sounded breathless, eager, even to herself. However, it was a woman friend of her mother's. Disappointment washed over her.

"Coryn? Is that you? It's Lucy Prentis. Is your mother on her way?" Her voice sounded extremely annoyed. "We've been waiting forty-five minutes."

"On her way?" Coryn repeated vaguely.

"Yes, of course." The irritation in Mrs. Prentis's voice increased. "This is our bridge day. The four of us have been playing bridge twice a month for nearly fifteen years. This is the second time your mother hasn't shown up."

Coryn felt a nervous flutter in her stomach. "She

isn't here, Mrs. Prentis. Maybe she had an appointment…I really don't know."

"An appointment? None of us ever make an appointment on our bridge day." The woman's tone was full of exasperation. "I simply don't understand it, Coryn. She could have at least called so we could have gotten a substitute. As it is…we've wasted another—"

"I'm sorry, Mrs. Prentis."

"Never mind. It's not your fault. I just wish if Clare has something else she'd rather do on these days, she would say so. Not ruin it for all of us."

Coryn didn't know what to say. Lucy Prentis and her mother had been close friends for as long as she could remember. It seemed odd that her mother would have forgotten a long-standing bridge date. Then she felt that elevator-drop feeling in the pit of her stomach. Or was it so odd? Not in light of the other puzzling incidents Clare had exhibited in the time Coryn had been home.

"I'm sorry, Mrs. Prentis," Coryn said. "I'll tell Mom you called."

The phone clicked. Coryn could imagine the expression on Lucy Prentis's face as she went back to the bridge table to inform the other two ladies that Clare had done it again.

Coryn put down the receiver. She felt a kind of sick jolt. She'd been so self-absorbed lately, preoccupied, she hadn't been aware that her mother might be having problems again. As she stood thinking about it, the back door opened and Clare walked in wearing an old sweater, jeans, gardening gloves. Her face had a smudge of dirt on one cheek and she had on a battered canvas hat. Her eyes were bright, her cheeks flushed. Seeing Coryn, she smiled. "I've been planting bulbs. They'll be gorgeous in the spring, grape hyacinths and jonquils."

Coryn started to tell her about Mrs. Prentis's irate call but something held her back. Her mother looked so happy she didn't have the heart. She would find out soon enough. Lucy Prentis wasn't known for tact.

Her mother seemed perfectly normal. Coryn was lulled into thinking that some of this might have to do with menopause. When she looked up symptoms for this what she learned felt rather reassuring. The severity of problems depended on the individual woman.

For the next ten days Coryn's attention focused on her mother. But even under this alerted observation Clare seemed normal. She went about the house doing the usual things. Perhaps she was a little quieter, a little distant, but on the whole herself.

Late one afternoon her mother tapped on Coryn's bedroom door, leaned in to say she was leaving to go to the grocery store. An hour later when Coryn went downstairs she found Clare sitting in the kitchen, staring blankly, her eyes confused, her expression troubled. Her car keys and grocery list were on the table in front of her.

When Coryn came in, her mother looked at her. "Darling, the craziest thing, I can't remember where the grocery store is. I've driven around, but I keep turning down the wrong streets, I just don't know...." Her voice trailed off and she shook her head helplessly.

Coryn felt a clutching sensation. She seemed to go on automatic. Somehow her voice managed to sound steady as she asked, "Do you still shop at Reddi-Rite?"

"Yes, of course. I always have. That's what makes this so insane." Her mother was genuinely baffled.

Gathering herself together quickly, Coryn asked, "Well, don't worry, Mom. I'll drive you." She attempted a laugh. "I think I remember how to get there."

Clare still looked unconvinced. "I just don't know what's gotten into me lately. I feel so foolish." She sounded exasperated, but she didn't protest Coryn's offer to take her.

The supermarket where they had shopped for groceries for as long as Coryn could remember was only a short distance away. It was, however, nearly five o'clock and the parking lot was crowded with late shoppers and people shopping after work. Coryn finally found a space, pulled in and turned off the engine.

Instead of immediately getting out of the car, Clare remained sitting there. "Want me to go in and help you, Mom?" Coryn said after a moment.

"Oh, honey, I don't know. Suddenly, I'm not feeling so well. Would you shop for me?"

Again Coryn felt a rush of anxiety. "Sure, Mom. Give me your list. I'll make quick work of it."

Her mother fumbled in her handbag and brought out a long slip of paper, and gave it to Coryn.

"Will you be okay? Would you like me to get a cola out of the soft-drink dispenser for you to sip while I shop?"

"I'll be fine, dear. I'll just roll down the window, get some fresh air."

Inside the store, Coryn looked at the list and had another shock. Her mother's handwriting was almost illegible. The scribbled items staggered crookedly down the page. It was hardly coherent. She'd just have to play it by ear, Coryn decided, pocketing the list. She grabbed a cart and started down the first aisle.

She felt breathless, disoriented. If only she had someone to talk to about her mother. Someone objective and not as involved in the situation as her father, someone with whom she could discuss her worry. But who? Mark's name came to her. If anyone, he would be the one compassionate enough, sensible enough. Mark would be the one, if she told anyone...

It was then that she saw two familiar figures just ahead of her, Mark and Ginny. She started to hurry to catch up with them then stopped herself. She felt awkward. It had been over three weeks since that evening at their home that had seemed so comfortable, so mutually enjoyable. She'd hoped—no, more than that, *expected* him to make another date. For just the two of them to go out to dinner, where they could talk. She had felt they were on the brink of something to be explored.

Suddenly Coryn was stricken with feelings of insecurity. Maybe she'd read too much into their being together. She had felt happy and hopeful. She loved Ginny, too. Had already begun to imagine how she could make the little girl's life happier...create a home that would be what Ginny had said wistfully a dollhouse family should be—with a daddy *and* a mommy.

As Coryn hesitated, Ginny turned around, saw her and waved. "Hi, Coryn." She tugged on Mark's sleeve. "Look, Daddy, there's Coryn. Oh, Coryn, I have something so exciting to tell you!"

Was it Coryn's imagination, or did Mark look embarrassed? He had too honest a face to hide what he was feeling. He *did* seem ill at ease. Why?

Then the blow struck. Ginny's little face was flushed, her eyes alive with excitement. "Oh, Coryn, I got my kitten! Orange, like I wanted, 'cept she has little white paws. And I called her Sunny just like I said."

It took all Coryn's effort to keep from looking at Mark. The *three* of them were *supposed* to have gone to the animal shelter to help Ginny select a kitten. It was something Mark had talked to her about. Something they had planned to do together. *She* was the one who had persuaded Mark to allow Ginny to have a pet.

Swallowing her hurt, Coryn said, "Oh, I'm so happy for you, Ginny. I bet she's precious."

"She's in the car in a box. We couldn't bring her into the store."

"Ginny, you were going to pick out the right kind of kitty food," Mark said.

Coryn glanced at him. He was definitely uncomfortable. Had he forgotten he had asked her to go with them? Or had he just thought better of the idea? Thought better about everything?

Stupidly, she felt like bursting into tears. Something like this shouldn't throw her. People forgot appointments, arrangements, plans...every day. Well, some people did. But not Mark, a small voice inside her head taunted.

When Ginny had gone happily down the aisle on her proud-pet-owner errand, it left the two of them standing awkwardly. A few inches apart. Worlds apart.

"I've been assigned a special feature series," he told her finally. "Lots of research into local stuff. Lots of interviews, that sort of thing. I've been swamped. Haven't had much free time."

Coryn stiffened. He didn't need to make excuses. She got the message. He'd had second thoughts about them. He wasn't planning to see her again anytime soon. And to think, she had almost...

"That should be interesting." She kept her voice even. "I've been busy, too, working on updating my résumé," she said briskly, smiling brightly. "Trying to make myself irresistible to a prospective employer." The minute she had said that, she could have bitten her tongue. "Well, *employable* anyway."

A cheerful voice came over the store's PA system. "Howdy, shoppers. Today's smart shopper's specials are on canned whole-kernel corn and hearty salsa in aisle four. Thanks for shopping Reddi-Rite."

Ironic, Coryn thought, my heart is breaking in the

canned-foods department of the supermarket. She had to get away, yet she seemed rooted to the spot.

Coryn felt immensely thankful when Ginny came back with a large box of dry cat food and wedged it carefully beside the laundry detergent and cornflakes in Mark's cart.

"Well, I better get on with my shopping. Mother's waiting in the car for me," Coryn told Mark. "Bye, Ginny," she said to the little girl. Swiftly she wheeled her shopping cart around Mark's and rushed down the aisle, not looking back.

Well, she didn't need things spelled out. It couldn't be any clearer. She could read between the lines. She'd had plenty of practice, hadn't she? With Jason. She was smarter now. At least she had *thought* she was. Of course, Mark hadn't tried to con her, use her the way Jason had. He was putting it right on the line.

Mindlessly she put food items in her cart. How on earth she would make a dinner out of any of this she could only guess. She knew she had not gotten half the things on the unreadable grocery list. But it didn't matter. All that mattered was getting out of there as quickly as possible. Out of the store. Away from Mark.

She stood at the checkout counter, biting her lower lip nervously, praying he didn't finish his shopping and join the same line or the one opposite hers. Her face felt stiff and stretched.

How many times did it have to happen to her before she saw the light? Showing your true feelings only made you a target. Being honest meant getting hurt. She thought she'd learned. But Mark seemed so different…Mark seemed—oh, how did she know? She wasn't good at reading people. Hadn't experience taught her that, if nothing else?

"We're all in this alone," comedian Lily Tomlin had quipped. Maybe that was true. You couldn't count on anyone. Trust anyone. How could she have forgotten that? Been crazy enough to hope?

Oh, why was the woman ahead of her being so slow? Coryn tapped her foot impatiently. The woman was carrying on a long explanation with the clerk about getting the wrong kind of dishwashing detergent. The clerk was sending the bag boy back down the store to exchange it for the right one. More delay. Coryn began to feel hot, choked. Exasperated. Desperate.

Out of the corner of her eye she thought she saw Mark and Ginny approach. She looked down into her cart, as though seeing if everything was there. Finally, the line moved. She unloaded her items onto the counter. The cash register was clicking. The clerk said something she didn't hear, she got out her wallet, hand poised to pull out the necessary bills. Thank goodness, at last. Her purchases were bagged, put back into the shopping cart and she rolled it toward the exit door.

Outside, the rush of cold air in her face revived her. Then she heard a voice behind her. "Miss, miss…"

She whirled around.

"Your change, miss." It was the bag boy. "You forgot your change."

"Oh, thank you," she said, thrusting the money into the pocket of her jacket. She stowed the groceries in the trunk of the car.

It was only when she was behind the wheel, fastening her seat belt that she realized her mother was no longer on the passenger side. Her heart literally stopped. She turned cold. Where in the world was she?

It was getting dark now and the shopping center was crowded with shoppers, cars. Coryn pulled the keys out of the ignition and got out of the car. Standing beside it she looked around frantically. Which way could Clare have gone? Breathing hard, Coryn walked back toward the Reddi-Rite entrance.

People in a hurry pushed loaded carts out through the automatic doors. No sign of her mother there. Should she go right or left? A number of smaller stores flanked the large grocery building. She couldn't have got too far, Coryn told herself. She'd only been in the store fifteen, twenty minutes.

Her heart hammered as she hurried down the sidewalk, checking the entryway into each store along the way. Then she saw her mother. She was standing in front of the display window of the variety store at the end of the block. Weak with relief, Coryn hurried toward her.

"Mom!" she said, grabbing her arm. "You scared me half to death. I didn't know where you were—"

Her mother turned to her with a wide-eyed stare. "Why, honey, I'm sorry...I just was doing a little window-shopping. Look at that dear little carousel.

Isn't that sweet? Wouldn't that make a darling gift for Mark Emery's little girl?"

The mention of Ginny was like salt in an open wound. She was still smarting from the hurt of what had just happened. Her own pain caused her voice to be sharp. "I don't know, Mom." She tugged at her coat sleeve. "Come on. It's late and we better get home before Dad. He'll be worried." He'd be even more worried if he knew about today, Coryn thought. She put her hand through her mother's arm and led her back to the car.

Dear God, what next?

Coryn was taking deep breaths as she got back in the car and slid behind the wheel. Her hand shook as she inserted her key into the ignition. Pulling out of her space, she went forward to make the turn into the highway, and saw Mark's station wagon. Foolish tears stung her eyes. She remembered an especially happy time they were all together. On their way home from the beach...singing.

It hurt, but then, she'd been hurt before. It was her own fault. Expecting too much, taking too much for granted.

Well, what had she expected? To dump on Mark right there in the middle of the canned section between sliced pineapple and cream of chicken soup? To tell him how worried she was about her mother? And even if she had and he had listened sympathetically because he liked her mother, what could he do? She would just have made him uncomfortable. People only listen to other people's troubles if they have to, or if they're paid to. That's all they can do, for fifteen minutes or an hour, at most. Then they go their own way, back to their own lives, feeling relieved that your problem, the one they've just heard about, isn't theirs. It's as if troubles or disasters were somehow contagious. If you get too close to one, you might contract it yourself.

Oh, I don't blame you, Mark, Coryn thought as she turned into the driveway. I wouldn't want to hear about this, either. If I had a choice. Which I don't.

"God help me," she prayed aloud as she got out of the car. Saying it, she knew only He could.

February

Chapter Fifteen

The next two days passed in an agony of indecision for Coryn. There was no use denying it any longer, there was something seriously wrong with her mother. She had to find out what. Dr. Roger Iverson had been their family physician as long as she could remember. Surely her mother had gone for a yearly physical checkup at least. Maybe she had told him about some of these memory lapses, the headaches, the lack of usual interest and energy. Certainly he could prescribe something that would help her. A mood elevator or maybe just some super vitamins.

The only way to find out was to make an appointment with him and talk to him herself. She planned to do it as soon as possible.

Coupled with this new worry was the disappointment about Mark Emery. The shattering of her brief hope for new happiness.

Both these things weighed heavily on Coryn's heart early that February morning when she came into the kitchen. Her father was alone. He put down the paper. "Good morning, hon. Your mother's sleeping in. Would you do a favor for me? Stop at the cleaners? Tonight's the banquet at the Highland Inn and they've got the suit I want to wear. Your mother was supposed to pick it up yesterday but evidently forgot."

"Sure, Dad," Coryn said quickly. Her father was frowning as if annoyed at another incident of her mother's memory slips.

Coryn again considered discussing her concerns about her mother with him. But he seemed so preoccupied and even a bit on edge this morning. He focused on the banquet, she realized.

The banquet was the annual fund-raising event for the benefit of the local heart association. Her father had reserved a table for them and some friends. Coryn had also forgotten about it. Even though it wasn't a blatantly political event, she knew by now that her father would be doing some networking there.

Later that morning, Coryn drove to the nearby small shopping mall where Wilson Dry Cleaners was located. The Dodges had been customers there for years. Both husband and wife worked in the establishment. When Coryn walked in, Mrs. Wilson was at the counter waiting on someone else.

After she finished with him, she turned to Coryn. "You've come to pick up your father's cleaning, right? It's been here over a week. I called and left a message for your mother but I guess she doesn't remember."

Mrs. Wilson cast a sympathetic glance at Coryn then went to the rotating clothes rack. After spinning it around a few times, examining tags, she took down two plastic bags and brought them back to the counter.

As she removed the sales slips and rang up the amount on the cash register, she said, "I'm glad you're back in Rockport, Coryn. I'm sure it's a comfort to your dad to have someone looking out for your mom these days."

She shook her head. "Such a pity." She glanced over both shoulders then leaned closer, lowered her voice. "Let me tell you, I know what it's like. I grew up with it. Both my parents were alcoholics, and it was tough."

Coryn pulled out her wallet and extracted two bills. Her ears rang. She couldn't believe what Mrs. Wilson had just said. What she was implying! Coryn felt her face flush hotly, then the blood drained from her head. Everything buzzed around her. The smell of the steam irons, the rhythmic slap of the mangles came from the back of the shop, Mrs. Wilson's flat voice merged into a droning hum. Coryn held out one icy hand for the change the woman was counting out, then turned and practically ran out of the store.

Back in the car, she sat very still for a long time. The old saying "It takes one to know one" sprang into Coryn's mind. Mrs. Wilson had somehow got the idea *her mother* was an alcoholic? That was idiotic. Her mother hardly ever touched liquor. To be identified as an alcoholic was outrageous. How had Mrs. Wilson ever got an idea like that?

* * *

The banquet room of the Highland Inn was filled with people. Elegantly gowned women chatted together. Men in dinner jackets streamed back and forth from the bar to their tables. The who's who of Rockport always turned out for this event. Dignitaries, aware of the importance of being seen at these community affairs, greeted people as they made their way to the head table; the mayor, members of the board of supervisors, directors of the Rockport Chamber of Commerce.

As Coryn entered with her parents, she saw Mark sitting at the press table. For a moment their glances locked. Coryn felt heat begin to rise into her face. She nodded. A brief smile touched her lips. These weeks of silence from Mark had renewed Coryn's resolve made after Jason, not to let herself be vulnerable to any man. Yet, she had let it happen again. Mark—and let's face it, Ginny—had become important to her. The hurt she now felt was doubly bitter.

As they made their way to their reserved table, her father was stopped several times by well-wishers. "Go for it, Neil!" and "Let me know when you decide. I want to help." These and other such remarks made Coryn realize her father was much more intent on running for the state assembly than she had assumed.

Coryn glanced at her mother. She looked lovely as usual, perfectly groomed except...before they left the house, Coryn had noticed that Clare was wearing two different-colored shoes. When she had called it to her attention, her mother had been embarrassed.

Coryn had downplayed the incident and her father had not been aware of it. She was glad she'd made the appointment with Dr. Iverson. There must be a reason for all this.

When her father's conversation with someone seemed to be dragging on, Coryn felt her mother's thin fingers clutch her arm and she turned to look at her. Clare's lips were pressed tightly together and her eyes were wide and frightened. She looked almost ill. Alarmed, Coryn asked, "Mom, are you okay?"

"Yes, dear, fine. Just a little dizzy for a moment." They had reached their table and Coryn helped her to a seat. With a shaky hand, her mother lifted the water glass and took a few sips. What had caused this—whatever it was—panic attack? Was it something someone had said? Didn't Clare want her husband to run for public office?

Under any other circumstances Coryn thought her mother would make the perfect politician's wife, beautiful, gracious, with all the social skills to charm constituents.

Feeling protective, Coryn took a seat beside Clare. Two other couples, old friends of the family, came to the table to join them. Immediately the conversation became general and lively. Neil came last. He was smiling broadly and seemed excited. Obviously he enjoyed all the attention. Knowing him as she did, Coryn knew her father considered the prospect of taking on the incumbent assemblyman a challenge, one he would assume with pleasure. But if her mother's problems were serious or got worse? The question hung unanswered in Coryn's mind.

Coryn glanced at Clare again. She seemed to have regained her composure. She and Lucy Prentis were discussing the Friends of the Library plans to fund the new reference room at the main library. For the moment she seemed all right. Relieved, Coryn sighed.

With conversations going at full tilt on either side of her, Coryn had a chance to look around the room. The press table was in her direct line of vision. It was disconcerting to realize that Mark was seated so he could observe her, which he was doing at the moment.

She felt uncomfortable. Conscious of Mark's regard, she lowered her eyes and looked down at the salad the waitress had just placed before her. Maybe she wouldn't feel so bad about it if she knew exactly why Mark had cooled.

A spattering of applause brought her back to the present. Don Moore, the president of the chamber of commerce was at the mike.

"Tonight I'd like to introduce some of our prominent citizens who are here supporting this project. These are people we all know and love because they are always there, ready to be counted on for whatever will help our county."

One by one he announced names, and people at various tables stood up to enthusiastic applause. Then Don Moore said, "Neil Dodge, who we hope is going to answer a groundswell of support to be our next north-coast assemblyman at the state legislature." Her father rose to his feet.

Everyone at their table began to clap loudly. There

were exclamations from every corner of the room as her father smiled and waved his hand. The applause went on for a long time until Neil sat down. There was a buzz of congratulatory comment from all sides. Glancing at her mother, Coryn saw her face had turned deathly pale. A few minutes later, Clare murmured something and struggled to get up from her chair. She stumbled slightly, sat down again. Then, with great effort, she rose, steadied herself on the back of the chair and started toward the exit into the lobby.

Coryn's father, deep in conversation with the man to his left, did not see her mother leave. With growing concern, Coryn watched Clare's progress across the room. She was weaving visibly. A stab of fear pierced Coryn's heart. She put down her napkin and darted a quick look at her mother's place. Her wineglass was untouched. She looked back at Clare. She was definitely wobbling. Quickly, Coryn pushed back her chair and walked to her side.

Taking firm hold of her mother's arm, she whispered, "Lean on me, Mom."

Swaying slightly, Clare leaned against her. Slowly they moved forward. As they did, Mark Emery suddenly appeared on the other side of her. Holding her arm steadily, he walked with them out the door into the lobby. There they eased Clare into one of the velvet chairs.

She raised her hand and passed it wearily across her forehead, murmured, "Thank you." She closed her eyes for a few seconds. "I don't know what came over me. I felt so dizzy."

"It's terribly hot in there," Mark said quickly. "All that crowd and noise. I felt a little woozy myself."

Clare looked relieved, and Coryn shot him a grateful glance.

"Let me get you some water," Mark offered, then left to do so.

"Do you want me to take you home, Mom?" Coryn asked.

Alarmed, Clare said, "Oh, no, I'll have to go back. Your father will be upset if I don't."

"You don't have to, Mom. Not if you don't feel well."

"I'll be fine. Just give me a few minutes."

"You're sure?"

"Yes, dear. Honestly."

Mark came back with a glass of water, handed it to Clare.

She took it with her hand visibly shaking. "Thank you, Mr. Emery. You're very kind."

Mark stood there, an anxious frown on his face. He glanced at Coryn, thinking she looked especially lovely tonight. She was wearing the same deep blue dress she'd had on the day of the New Year's open house. She seemed unconscious of his presence. She was concentrating totally on her mother. He sensed her distress, longed to reach out, touch her, say something comforting.

Coryn felt Mark's gaze upon her and tensed. The situation could not have been more awkward. This was the first time they'd been in each other's presence since that awful day in the supermarket. Coryn felt embarrassed yet aware of his sensitivity, coming to their aid as he had. It was that very quality in him that had drawn her to him. It had caused her to let down her defenses, to dream, to hope. Almost tongue-tied with nervousness, Coryn murmured, "Yes, thank you."

Whatever Mark was feeling, he said, "Not at all. Gave me a chance to skip the rest of those boring speeches." He grinned. "I had to leave to go by the paper anyway."

He paused, then asked Coryn, "Is your father really planning to run for the assembly?"

"I guess he's thinking seriously about it." She glanced at her mother apprehensively. But she seemed her calm, poised self once more.

"I'd like to have an interview. That is, when he's ready."

"I'll tell him," Coryn replied.

"Well, I'll say good-night to you both. I hope you feel better, Mrs. Dodge."

"Oh, I'm fine now. Thank you again, Mr. Emery." Clare smiled her brilliant smile.

After Mark left, Coryn asked, "Ready?"

"Yes, darling, ready." Her mother seemed completely restored. "Ready to face the roaring lions in the den." She slipped her hand through Coryn's arm, pressed it slightly. "Don't mention my little spell to your dad. He'd worry. Unnecessarily. He's got so much on his mind just now."

They went back to their places at the table. Coryn glanced around. No one seemed to have missed them or noted their return. Coryn would have felt less at ease if she had known their table companions were purposely avoiding mentioning their sudden departure, that curious eyes had followed them as they had made their way to the lobby, and suspicious whispers on wagging tongues had spread malicious rumors from table to table.

Chapter Sixteen

The day of Coryn's appointment with Dr. Iverson, she felt nervous. Now that she had arranged to see the doctor, she was afraid of what he would tell her. At least, maybe after talking with him, she'd be able to get some handle on what was wrong with her mother.

She hadn't wanted to go during his regular office hours. In order for the doctor to see a reasonable number of patients, the patient flow had to be kept moving. Conscious of the necessity of keeping each visit to twenty minutes, the nurse moved patients quickly from waiting room to examining room. To avoid this, Coryn requested an after-hours appointment. When the doctor's secretary had attempted to elicit the nature of the visit, Coryn had used her most assertive tone. "It's a personal matter. I'm sure if you give Dr. Iverson my name and tell him that I'll come at the most convenient time for him *after* his last appointment, he will see me."

She was put on hold, and a few minutes later the secretary came back on the line. "If you can be here at five fifteen sharp, Dr. Iverson will see you."

Long before it was time for her to leave the house and drive downtown, Coryn was dressed and ready to go. Wondering how to fill up the time before she had to leave, she paced restlessly. Then the phone rang. She grabbed it on the second ring. In reply to her greeting she heard Mark's voice.

"Coryn?"

For him to call today, of all days was a shock. After all the days she had hoped and waited in vain for his call coming now was an anti-climax. That encounter in the supermarket had hurt badly. But she had already accepted that their brief romance was over. Regretted it, but had determined to recover. Instinctively, she steeled herself from letting her hopes be stirred up again.

"Coryn, I've been thinking about you, thought about calling several times, but—" he broke off, then, "What I'm calling about is that I'd like to see you. I *want* to see you. I feel—I mean I know I owe you an explanation—"

Coryn cut in. "Not at all, Mark," her voice sounding sharper than she intended. "You don't owe me anything."

"I feel I do," he said firmly, quietly. "Could we meet? I'd like a chance to talk."

She hesitated. Why was he starting this up again? Mixed feelings churned. Why *now* when she was just getting over him? She hesitated. His voice came again, "Please, Coryn, it's important."

"Well," she still hesitated. Why put herself through another emotional scene? Yet, something within her wanted to hear what Mark had to say, what kind of explanation, excuse was he going to give. What harm was there in that? "I have an appointment downtown at five," she countered.

He jumped at that. "Great. Then we could meet at the little espresso place on the square."

She knew the one he was talking about. They'd met there before. It was right across from the newspaper. The Medical Arts building where Dr. Iverson's office was close by.

"All right. In about an hour?"

"I'll be there. Thanks," Mark said and hung up.

To her chagrin she arrived first. She found a table and sat down. Out the window she could see the front of the newspaper building. She could also see children playing around the fountain in the middle of the square, young mothers pushing strollers, couples walking hand in hand. Watching, she felt a thrust of nostalgia, a yearning to somehow trade places with any of them, a deep longing for something she had never had, possibly never would...

"Sorry to keep you waiting. Something came up just as I was leaving—"

Startled, she looked up. It was Mark. His hair was windblown, his tie askew, the collar of his corduroy jacket turned up.

"It's okay."

"I'll get our coffee," he said and walked over to the counter.

Coryn turned away, looked out the window again.

The couple she had seen before were kissing. She felt a hard lump in her throat. Why had she come here? Why put herself through whatever Mark was going to say? Could she just get up and walk out? Leave before he came back to the table?

She heard the hiss of the espresso machine, smelled the warm scent of coffee, chocolate, cinnamon.

"Here we go." Mark was back, carefully placing the glass cup in its metal holder, containing the fragrant foamy brew, in front of her.

"Thanks for coming," he said in a low voice. "I really wanted to talk to you—needed to."

"It wasn't necessary, Mark, I told you on the phone."

"Look, Coryn, allow me this. It may not seem necessary to you but it is to me. I feel I've let you down and it wasn't fair because it had nothing to do with you. It was me. My fault." He paused, lowered his voice. "So that you understand, I have to go back to when Shari died. That first year afterward was rough going for both Ginny and me. I was so devastated, I wasn't much good for anything, mostly not for her as the parent she needed so desperately. When the shock started to wear off and I got myself together again, I decided to make her my priority in life. Concentrate on being a good father—being everything to her. We had a shaky start but finally we somehow got our life together. We moved up here and a kind of pattern was established. I began to think I had to stay the course, so to speak. To add another factor—a third person into our life wouldn't be a good idea." Mark's hands were clenched together on the table, so tightly the knuckles were pale. "That's why, when I found myself attracted to you, I got scared—asked myself was I ready? Was Ginny ready? Relationships take time, concentration, to build, develop—" he sighed heavily, "That's what I wanted to explain. It had nothing to do with you, actually. You've been wonderful. Ginny is crazy about you. She asks about you all the time. Then, when we saw you in the supermarket that day, I realized...I'd let you down. Hurt you without meaning to. And I'm sorry, Coryn. I'm truly..."

Coryn felt her heart throbbing in her throat. She couldn't take any more of this. It was too late for Mark to be telling her all this. Too late for his apologies, however heartfelt. She didn't need to hear them. Not now. She gathered up her purse and said, "Mark, I have to go. I have an appointment—" she got up and he put his hand on her arm.

"Wait, Coryn, do you understand what I'm saying?"

She shook her head. "Mark, my life is very complicated right now. I'm sorry. I have to go."

She rushed out of the café and outside the brisk wind was cold and she shivered. Her vision blurred by unshed tears, she walked quickly toward the Medical Arts building.

It was all just too much. There might have been a time, not too long ago when she could have listened, accepted what he was saying, but not now. She had enough to deal with.

She had to focus on her mother now and get to

the bottom of this mystery. She pushed through the glass doors of the medical office building, she pushed aside all thoughts of Mark. She hurried through the lobby and caught an elevator before its doors were about to close.

When Coryn arrived at Dr. Iverson's office the waiting room was empty. She could see his office staff behind the glass enclosure turning off computers, putting folders into file cabinets, clearing off their desks. Nervously, Coryn sat down, automatically straightened some magazines on the low table in front of it.

Soon, the door opened and Dr. Iverson, wearing a white lab jacket, stuck his head in. "Hello, Coryn, come on in."

Roger Iverson was a tall, lean man with a deeply lined face, thick steel-gray hair, kind eyes behind rimless glasses. He held the door for her and she entered the hallway that led to his office at the end. Someone called his name, and he stopped to sign something on a clipboard one of the nurses brought to him. "Good night, Doctor," she said, and gave Coryn a curious glance before retracing her steps to the glass-enclosed space.

Dr. Iverson shut the office door and indicated the leather armchair opposite his desk. "Sit down, Coryn. I'm glad you came. It's about your mother, isn't it?"

Coryn's heart gave a surprised little jump. She nodded as Dr. Iverson settled his tall frame in the swivel chair behind his desk. She watched as he reached for a manila folder, placed it in front of him and opened it. Then he clasped his hands together and looked over at her.

Coryn swallowed, her throat suddenly dry. Instinctively she knew that whatever he was about to say would change things forever.

So she began to talk, chatter really, as if to delay what eventually he was going to tell her. "Yes, Dr. Iverson. Since I've come home, I've noticed some changes in her that are puzzling, so unlike her. I mean, she seems confused, uncertain, forgetful. I think she's depressed, she's not herself at all. I just thought maybe you could give her something that might help—a prescription or—maybe she should see a psychiatrist…" Coryn's voice trailed off faintly as Dr. Iverson's gaze met hers steadily.

He shook his head slowly. "Your mother doesn't need a psychiatrist, Coryn. If it would help, I would have suggested it. Normally, I wouldn't disclose this kind of information without a patient's permission. But I've known your family for so long. And knowing the type of person your mother is, perhaps I should tell you everything."

"Tell me what, Doctor?" Coryn pressed him.

"I'm sorry to have to tell you this, but we've already made some tests. She came to me herself several months ago. She didn't want Neil to know but she was worried about herself. Although she tried to downplay the situation. You know how Clare is. She even made it sound slightly humorous…mentioning her forgetfulness, some incident or other that was funny—if it weren't so symptomatic of what her trouble is."

Coryn sat forward in her chair. "And that is?"

"Your mother is in the initial stages of Alzheimer's."

"Alzheimer's," Coryn repeated woodenly.

"You must have heard or read about it."

She had, of course. Alzheimer's. The disease of a former president and a glamorous movie star of the fifties. But it was an old people's disease. Her mother was barely fifty. An image of vague eyes, tottering people on walkers or in wheelchairs, heads drooping, bodies slumped. The image had no connection with her beautiful mother.

While Coryn sat frozen, her hands clenched tightly in her lap, Dr. Iverson's voice went on as if coming from a long distance.

"Alzheimer's is a progressive disease. It is, so far, incurable. The patient deteriorates to the point of being helpless. Unable to remember places, events, people. Unable to even recognize family members, or dress or feed themselves." He hesitated, then said, "This is hard for me to tell you, Coryn. I tried to talk to Neil about it not long ago. But he is in denial. He doesn't want to hear this. No one could blame him. It isn't the kind of diagnosis a doctor wants to give to a family. Especially not to friends. I've known Clare as long as I've known you." Dr. Iverson shook his head. "He has to know, Coryn. He has to be told and he has to accept it. I guess it's up to you."

Her lips pressed close together, she nodded. "What can I do?"

"I suggest you learn as much as you can about

this disease. That way you'll know what is ahead for you as your mother's condition worsens. At least it will prepare you for what to look for, what to expect. And you can help your father.''

It was already dark when Coryn left Dr. Iverson's office. She drove slowly, but when she nearly turned twice into a one-way street, she knew she shouldn't be driving at all in her state of mind. She pulled to the side of the road and sat there for a few minutes taking deep breaths. It was all so unreal. And yet it was happening. She had to go home, somehow tell her father.

After a while she turned on the engine, started her car and drove the rest of the way home.

Coming into the house she saw the light in her father's den. The rest of the house was in darkness. She walked through the house turning on lamps as she went. At his den door she halted.

''Dad? Anything wrong?'' the words were out of her mouth before she realized she'd said them. Momentarily she forgot *she* was the one with the bad news.

Her father lifted his head from his desk. His face was drawn, his eyes were circled with shadows, the lines around his mouth seemed to have deepened since she had seen him that morning.

''Hello, honey. You're late. Been shopping?'' He tried a smile.

She shook her head. ''Where's Mom?''

''Oh, she had a slight headache. Went up to bed.''

Coryn felt she had to sit down. Her legs seemed suddenly to have lost their strength.

Her father looked at her, frowning. ''What is it? You look—I don't know—worried.''

"Dad, I have something to tell you. Something you have to know," she said. "I've just come from Dr. Iverson's office and—"

"You're not sick, are you?" her father asked, concerned.

"No, Dad, not me. It's Mother I went to see him about. Surely you've noticed that there have been changes. Things you've mentioned yourself, like her leaving the stove burners on, that sort of thing. Well, she's sick, Dad. Very sick. Seriously sick."

He closed his eyes, looking pained.

"I know you don't want to hear this, Dad." Coryn's voice broke. "But it's something we can't deny any longer."

"I know." Her father spoke heavily. "I guess I've known for months, just didn't want to admit it was anything but maybe...a woman her age goes through changes."

"It's more than that, Dad. It's Alzheimer's. Dr. Iverson confirmed it. We can't ignore it."

Her father rubbed his hand across his forehead wearily and then, almost as if speaking to himself, he said, "One day a few months ago, before Thanksgiving, before you came home, she went out to do some errands...ordinary things, things she's always done, grocery shopping, taking clothes to the cleaners, getting gas for her car—" He halted, his expression was anguished. "Mike, at the service station, told me that not fifteen minutes after he'd filled her tank, checked the oil and tires, she came back. Evidently didn't remember she'd already been there. He made a joke of it. But I tell you, Coryn, it made my heart stop. She shouldn't be driving in her condition.

"Then, coming home one evening and finding her still in her bathrobe, sitting at the table in the kitchen staring out the window, the breakfast dishes still on the table. When she saw me, she was amazed... *what was I doing home?* She couldn't believe it was five o'clock. The whole day had passed and she wasn't even aware of it.

"I wrestled with that incident not knowing exactly what to think or do." He got up and started pacing. "I didn't want to alarm her. Every time something like that happened, she got so upset, apologetic... as though it were her fault, as if I were blaming her. I thought with you here, things would get better. That maybe she felt isolated, useless, lonely in this big house... you know, the empty-nest syndrome. Maybe, that she was depressed."

"I suggested that to Dr. Iverson," Coryn interrupted. "Asked him if seeing a psychiatrist might help, but he said—" Her father stopped pacing and looked directly at her. Hope seemed to leap into his eyes. Coryn shook her head slightly. "He told me a psychiatrist can't help Alzheimer's victims. It's a disease of the central nervous system. Not emotional, psychotic or neurotic." Coryn bit her lower lip, struggling to go on. "She won't get any better, she'll get steadily worse. She won't recognize us..."

Her father sat down again, put his head in his hands. "Oh, no dear God, no!" Then he mumbled, "Is Dr. Iverson sure?"

"Yes, Dad. There isn't any doubt."

Her father's face seemed to crumble, and he buried his head in his hands again. Hearing the wracking sobs, seeing the broad shoulders shake, Coryn watched helplessly. She had never heard a man cry before. Certainly not her father. It was heart-wrenching. It was something she would never forget.

Tears ran down her own cheeks. She reached out her hand and placed it on his arm. "Dad, I'm so sorry, so very sorry."

He groped for her hand, clutched it. "I can't go through this alone, Coryn. I need you. Will you stay? Help me through this?"

"Yes, Dad, of course. I'll do whatever I can." Coryn tried to sound reassuring. She knew she was walking into a dark tunnel the end of which she couldn't see, even if there might be a light there.

They talked quietly for a half hour or so. Her father looked so drained, so weary, Coryn persuaded him he should go to bed, get some rest.

As he left, she gave him a hug, patted his shoulder. "Try not to worry too much, Dad. I'll be here for Mom—for both of you..."

"I know you will, sweetheart. I appreciate that."

Coryn watched him cross the hall to the foot of the stairway. His step was slow, his shoulders sagged visibly. She realized she was holding her breath.

She turned back into the room. The fire in the hearth sputtered, the logs crumbled to a blaze of glowing embers. Dr. Iverson had finally answered Coryn's questions about her mother's behavior. But it was not the answer she'd wanted to hear.

"I can't go through this alone, Coryn," her father

had said. But could she really help? *She* desperately needed someone to talk with about this awful thing that had attacked her mother, invaded their family life.

The thought of Mark came to her but just as quickly left. Not now. If things had worked out for them it might be different. He had known tragedy himself, would understand. Even as that possibility fleetingly came and went, the words of an old country song came into her mind. A plaintive ballad they all used to sing in the car on their way to go camping when she was a child. Her dad would put on a throbbing twang as he sang it. The lyrics spoke so poignantly about walking in a lonesome valley. Walking it by yourself.

Did everyone have to walk some lonesome valley by themselves in life? Was this hers?

Chapter Seventeen

A week later, on a cold, rainy night, Coryn and her parents were just finishing dinner, when the phone rang. Neil answered it. "I see. In about twenty minutes? Sure, that will be fine." Her father put down the receiver and came back to the table with an odd expression on his face. "That was Mark Emery. He asked if he could come over this evening."

"I think he wants to interview you," Coryn said, feeling guilty she'd forgotten to mention that to her father. Since that painfully awkward incident at the supermarket and her meeting with Dr. Iverson, she'd had other things on her mind. "He said something about wanting to when we saw him at the inn the other evening." She glanced at her mother for confirmation. But she was rearranging the flowers in the centerpiece, not paying attention to this exchange between her husband and daughter. Her father frowned. "Maybe it's something Glenn set up."

Coryn knew one of her father's old friends, Glenn

Ackerman, was actively working on a grassroots organization to support her father for the assembly seat. She was sure her father had not yet given an official okay. *Was* he going ahead with this? Even now that he knew her mother's diagnosis? Coryn looked questioningly at him. He was looking at his wife, his frown deepening. What was he thinking? Was some part of him still in denial? Didn't he see the things Clare did? Hadn't he noticed the slippage? Clare was not quite so careful about her grooming, got her colors mixed up and sometimes did not have her usual carefully coordinated look. Then there were non sequiturs, the sentences that broke off in the middle, the random remarks that went nowhere, the tendency to stare off into space.

Tension gripped Coryn, tightening her stomach muscles. Her father seemed to have been totally unaware of what had happened at the banquet a week ago. Was he the only one who had not noticed Clare's shaky exit, her lack of balance? Mark had certainly noticed. There had been something in the look he had given her that made Coryn certain *he* knew...at least knew *something* was wrong.

Her mother's soft voice interjected itself into Coryn's uneasy thoughts. "I think I'll go up, if you two will excuse me. There's an old movie on TV, *Portrait of Jenny*—I loved it when I saw it as a teenager. I think I'll just curl up in bed and watch it."

"You don't want to wait and see Mark Emery?" Neil said.

"He just wants to talk politics with you, dear." She smiled at her husband. She got up, leaned over and kissed him, patted Coryn on the cheek as she passed her and floated out of the room.

The phone rang again and automatically her father picked it up. He was soon involved in a conversation. Coryn wondered if she should stay or not. Was her mother right? Was it just politics Mark wanted to discuss? Or was he coming for the interview he said he wanted? If so, she wondered why he hadn't arranged a meeting at her father's office.

Her father was still on the phone when the front doorbell chimed. Coryn would have to answer it. She rose from her chair and started walking toward the hall. Ranger, who had been drowsing in front of the fireplace, got stiffly to his feet and followed her.

Conscious of her inner nervousness, Coryn told herself, *Don't be silly.* Mark was coming to see her father, not her. She opened the door.

"Good evening, Coryn."

"Come in. My father's on the phone but he should be off in a few minutes."

Ranger wagged his tail and Mark bent to smooth the dog's head. "Hiyah, fella." He looked at Coryn. "Great dog."

"Yes, he is," she said. "Here, let me take your coat."

They went into the living room. Her father, having completed his conversation, joined them. He came forward, extending his hand to Mark. "Good to see you," he said heartily. "Can I offer you some coffee?"

"No, thank you, sir. This isn't a social visit exactly." Mark stood rubbing his hands together as if to warm them.

"An interview, then?"

"Not that, either—" Mark hesitated, as if uncertain how to proceed. He glanced at Coryn. For help? she wondered. "Maybe I should leave," she said.

"Not at all," Mark said. "I think you should stay. Hear what I've come to say to your father."

Suddenly the atmosphere in the room changed. This was something important. Something that couldn't be put off. Something they each needed to hear.

Coryn sat down on the edge of the sofa. Her father indicated Mark take one of the armchairs, and Neil sat down in the other. Mark leaned forward, clasped his hands in front of him.

Coryn had a good view of his face and as the moment lengthened before he began to speak, she had a chance to study it. She had seen it often at close range. It was a good face, an intelligent one of character and strength. She had seen how mobile it was. In it she had seen a number of expressions— tender and loving, as with Ginny, alert and intense when talking about something he believed in or cared deeply about. She had seen it briefly touched with sadness when he spoke of Shari, or alive with humor when he was amused.

"Mr. Dodge, I may be way out of line coming to you with this," Mark began. "I've given it a lot of thought and in the end, I had to. As a reporter in the community, I've watched you from a distance. I've also enjoyed the hospitality of your home and the company of your daughter. I don't think of myself as a close friend, but I do feel a responsibility to tell you what is being widely circulated and give you the option of addressing it."

"Well, go ahead, man. Whatever it is, say it."

"Of course, it is common knowledge you are seriously considering running for state office. You have plenty of support. But, much as I hate to say it, politics isn't lawn tennis, it's hardball. Anyone as visible and successful as you in any town has collected a few enemies as well as friends. I'm afraid your opponent is one of these, and his cronies are very adept at smear tactics and dirty tricks. Most politically ambitious people don't fully realize—some not until they're deep into it—that the family of the candidate is the easy target."

"What do you mean?" Neil demanded.

"I'm afraid there are some unfortunate rumors being circulated about—" Mark swallowed as if it was hard for him to speak "—about your wife, about Mrs. Dodge."

"What?" Coryn's father jumped up, anger reddening his face.

"Nothing about her character, sir. Anyone who knows her knows what a lovely—"

"Never mind. What are the rumors? What are people saying?"

"I'm sorry, sir. But they're saying she has a drinking problem, that she's an alcoholic."

Coryn's father muttered something under his breath. His hands clenched into fists. He paced the length of the living room and back two or three times before spinning around and facing Mark. "It's a lie. You know there isn't a shred of truth in it." He pounded one fist into his open palm. "She hardly ever has a sip of anything. Isn't that right, Coryn? Have you ever seen your mother even finish a glass of wine, for that matter? How dare they spread such a malicious falsehood!"

"I understand how you feel, Mr. Dodge. Some people will see it for what it is—an unscrupulous political tactic. But a lie told often enough begins to have a life of its own. One thing leads to another, something added here and there, and before you can stop it, it's too late. It's become a fact."

Coryn felt like someone struck by lightning. Mrs. Wilson's remarks at the dry cleaners. The scene at the Highland Inn banquet flashed back into Coryn's mind. How many people had witnessed it? If they had already heard the rumor, that incident was the evidence they needed to confirm suspicion.

"Mr. Dodge, your political enemies will not only use this to discredit Mrs. Dodge and to weaken your position. Some people will do anything, use anyone, to gain power. Family values is the name of the game right now. If they can insinuate any kind of dysfunction, addiction. *Anything* to win, they will." He paused. "I thought you ought to know. Then you can decide how to handle it."

Her father was chalk-white. The veins in his forehead stood out. His mouth was pressed into a tight, straight line. Coryn did not think she had ever seen her father so upset. He fought his anger silently. It was a battle he was waging against his own ambition, the evil intent of others to wound and injure someone he loved.

Coryn held her breath, observing the inner struggle. Gradually, she saw a change come over her father's face. The tense lines relaxed. His eyes refocused on Mark. In a quiet voice, he said, "I appreciate very much your coming here with this. It took courage to do so. Thank you." He waited a few minutes then asked, "What do you suggest?"

Mark seemed a little taken aback by that. "I hardly could advise you on that, Mr. Dodge, unless..."

"Unless what?"

"Unless I knew how much you wanted to run. How much it meant to you."

"Nothing means as much to me as my family." His voice was steady.

"And you have given consideration to what kind of strain a political campaign puts on the family?"

"Maybe not enough. It's been an exciting idea. Running, that is. I've succeeded at anything I've set my mind on doing. I could always count on Clare to—" He stopped abruptly. "She hasn't been well lately but..." He halted, glanced at Coryn.

"Dad," she remonstrated gently, reminding him of what Dr. Iverson had cautioned them both against. "Alzheimer's is a slow, progressive disease, but don't fool yourself, it doesn't get any better—it irrevocably goes its course."

Her father's whole body tensed dramatically. Coryn understood what this breach of family privacy cost him. Then he turned back to Mark. "The truth is, Clare is in the early stages of Alzheimer's. That may account for some of the rumors. She is some-times...not herself. There are symptoms. We may have grown used to them, but someone seeing her...unsteadiness, at times her confusion, her slurred speech, *might* think...'' He shook his head. ''It wouldn't be good, wouldn't be fair to expose her to the limelight, the scrutiny of people. I guess I hadn't really thought this through.''

His shoulders slumped. He sat back down.

''May I make a suggestion?'' Mark ventured.

''Yes, sure. What is it?''

''I think if I were you...whatever your decision is...whether to run or not, I would make a public statement. Come right out with it. Tell people of Clare's illness. Just what it is, how it affects its vic-tims. I'm sure there is hardly a family in this state who hasn't had someone, a parent, a relative, a spouse, afflicted with Alzheimer's. If you decide to run, your declaration would totally defeat any weapon the opponent had thought to use against you. If you decide not to, it would be a reasonable excuse to the people who wanted to support you. In either case, going public would gain you only sympathy and respect.''

A thoughtful silence followed. Mark got to his feet.

Coryn's father stood, too, held out his hand, clasped Mark's. ''Thank you for coming.''

''Not at all, sir. I am very fond of Mrs. Dodge. She has been gracious to me and my daughter. I hope things turn out for the best for all of you.'' Mark hesitated a moment, then said, "Well, I'll be on my way."

Her father did not move. It was almost as if he couldn't.

Mark glanced at Coryn. Their gazes held a moment, then Mark said, "Would you see me to the door?"

Startled, Coryn felt jerked like a puppet, knowing she should have simply done that without being asked. "Of course." Together they walked to the front door.

"I want you to know how sorry I am," Mark said.

Her mind still on "pause," Coryn stared at him. Sorry? Sorry for what? For her mom? For not calling her in all these week? She did not know what to say to that. "Thank you very much" was all she could manage.

"I wish I could do something to help."

"You have. I think you said exactly what my father needed to hear. He's been in denial. Maybe we both have."

Mark stood there for another moment as though he wanted to say something else. Then apparently he decided there was nothing he *could* say. "Well, good night then." He opened the door, then hand on the knob, turned. "If there *is* anything I can do. Anything at all…"

Her throat felt swollen. She could hardly get out the words. "Thanks, it's very kind of you."

"Coryn…"

He spoke her name softly. She felt tears stinging

at the back of her eyes. She wished he would go before she flung herself into his arms, sobbing.

The moment of uncertainty hovered, then Mark said, "Good night." This time he left.

She closed the front door and went slowly back into the living room. Her father was slumped in the armchair, one hand covered his eyes.

"Dad, I think Mark's right, don't you?" she asked gently.

"I *know* he's right. I don't know how I couldn't have seen it myself." He shook his head slowly. "Your poor mother. I've probably added to her problem. Couldn't see the forest for the trees. Or maybe I just didn't want to see. Mark Emery's right. I'll get a statement out tomorrow. I'll have him help me write it."

He paused, then, "He's a fine man. Not many people would have the guts to come right out and tell you something like this. I admire him a great deal." He pulled himself to his feet. "I think I'll go up now, see how Clare's doing."

He stood for a minute looking down at his daughter, then reached out and laid one hand on her head. "Thanks, honey, for sticking around. We'll get through this—whatever it is—together." He sighed heavily then left the room.

Coryn felt drained. Limp. Unable to move. The fire had dwindled to a mass of glowing coals. When she was a youngster, she had tried to find pictures there, imagining all sort of shapes and forms. Tonight it was only Mark's face she saw. In it she had seen compassion, understanding, empathy. Her father, not known to be particularly discerning, had seen something fine in Mark, too.

Mark was a rare human being. A man who could be trusted, a man who could be loved without risk of betrayal.

Coryn wasn't sure how long she remained in the living room alone. Her thoughts were jumbled, flitting from one thing to another. There was so much to think about. Some time later, Coryn banked the fire, went upstairs. The door to her parents' bedroom was slightly ajar as she passed it on her way to her own. She heard the low murmur of voices and glanced in. She saw her mother, in a pink satin nightgown and robe, sitting on the side of the bed. Her head was turned toward the TV set so that only her profile was visible. Her hair was down and fell away from her slender neck onto her shoulders, making her look touchingly young.

Her father was on his knees beside her taking off her slippers. His hand was holding her delicate instep almost in a caress. Coryn drew in her breath. The scene was intimate, one of devotion that found no task too menial or ordinary to do for the beloved.

Coryn felt almost embarrassed at inadvertently seeing such a tender scene. Yet she was moved deeply by it. It was as if it had been given her as a gift. To witness the love her father was showing.

In that moment, Coryn realized her father would not run for office and she realized the sacrifice he was making. Putting aside his own ambitions, his own plans, his own goals—that this was what true marriage was all about. It was what had held her parents together all these years. Their vows taken so long ago, neither knowing what might lie ahead, what they might be called upon to do. Those promises to each other had perhaps been spoken without any real understanding, but they were now being met with courage and faith.

Coryn felt her heart twist with love and admiration for these two she loved so dearly. She moved quietly by, seeking the refuge of her own room. What she had glimpsed was truth. The truth of a long, enduring love that met whatever challenges lay upon the path they had chosen to walk together.

Would she ever know such a love, or be able to give it? That kind of love was the key that opened a heart to pour out whatever was required. That was the kind of love she wanted, longed for, but that had so far eluded her.

March

Chapter Eighteen

Coryn's alarm clock buzzed persistently. Without opening her eyes, she reached out and shut it off. She lay there for a minute wondering why she had set it. Then slowly, like touching an aching tooth with her tongue, she remembered.

She dragged herself out of bed. She stumbled toward the bathroom to dash her face with water, brush her teeth, twist her hair up into a bun, secure it with an elastic ribbon. Dressing quickly in a sweater, pants, she tiptoed downstairs and out to her car.

It was still dark outside as Coryn drove to the community pool. She'd started going swimming every day, a therapy she'd discovered worked for her. She discovered the early morning gave her time before the rest of the day's duties faced her. She had taken on more and more of the jobs her mother used to handle so easily, so efficiently. It seemed to Coryn her mother was going steadily downhill. It frightened her, and swimming seemed to lessen the tension she felt.

She also used the time to pray. For strength, for courage, for whatever the next months held. In the last several weeks she had turned to prayer more than ever before in her life. They were not the quick, desperate prayers or the careless ones she had often prayed. These were different. She had felt more tuned in than ever before. They were a kind of listening prayer. Seeking strength, guidance. For the first time in her life she knew *she* had to be there for her parents the way they had always been there for her. It was a new role, one she hadn't expected, one she did not feel prepared for. The word *help* prayerfully said was often on her lips and in her mind and heart as she went through the day.

She parked her car, slung the bag containing her bathing suit, thongs, towel and toilette articles over her shoulder and went inside the pool building. At once the combined smells of chlorine, wet tile, canvas and plastic prickled her nostrils. She showed her pass card to be punched, got her locker key and went into the dressing room.

Earlier swimmers were already showering, using the hair dryers, chatting with one another. Coryn moved right to a locker, opened it, stowed her bag, started undressing. All around her women friends were discussing their weight, their diets, their husbands and children. She nodded to a few whom she recognized as regulars, but spoke to no one. The whole point of this self-prescribed therapy was her anonymity. She didn't want to speak to anyone or have anyone speak to her. She'd heard sharing burdens was helpful. She'd always heard that. But right now she knew that the only way she could bear this awful thing that was happening was not to talk about it. As if not talking about it made it not real.

She pulled on her tank suit, slipped her bare feet into thongs and moved like a robot into the prerequisite shower. Afterward she tossed her towel over her shoulder and walked down the green-painted corridor to the pool.

Aqua-tinted water shimmered from the painted bottom of the big, rectangular pool. Light from the gray day outside, filtered through the slanted windows, was augmented by glaring bulbs in aluminum fixtures set in the arched ceiling. A lifeguard sat at one end on a mounted place from where he could view the swimmers. Every sound was amplified in the enormous room. The ponging sound of the diving board's metal springs, the echoing splash as the diver hit the water. Coryn disliked the claustrophopic feeling of swimming indoors. She had always loved swimming in a mountain lake or in the ocean. Coryn bit her lip and struggled with the urge to leave. But she was here for a purpose. Necessary activity to combat stress-induced depression.

She shoved her hair into her bathing cap while looking for an empty lane. She went to the side of the pool. Suppressing the reluctance to get into the water, she sat down on the edge, dangled her feet in the water, shivering as the chill ripples swirled around her ankles. Finally, taking a deep breath, she pushed herself into the water.

There were two what she called "serious swimmers" in the lanes on either side of her. One was
doing a vigorous backstroke, the other a butterfly
crawl. Water spewed up in their wakes and Coryn
quickly ducked her head and slid into a slow breast-
stroke down to the other end of the pool.

At first it took just grim determination to swim the
length of the lane. She forced herself back and forth
a half-dozen times, alternating from sidestroke to
crawl then floating on her back, making her arms
propel her.

Gradually some of the tension began to drift away
as she concentrated on her swimming.

That was why she came here, to blank out the
shock, sadness, grief she felt about her mother's illness. The unfairness of it all would gnaw, and the
grinding pain would activate as she plowed through
the resisting water. Slowly the tears would come and
she would let them. No one saw or noticed. The marathon swimming went on on either side of her.

Kicking her feet, arms pulling strongly with each
stroke, she fought back the terror of what they might
be facing further along. Here she could let the tears
she dared not cry at home in the presence of either
parent flow. Running in rivulets down her cheeks and
no one would see. She could swim under the surface
of the water, come up, her face wet. Nobody paid
any attention. Everyone was here for single-minded
fitness goals, exercise, physical training.

She turned the panic into energy. The fear. She
had to admit she was afraid. Afraid of what she might
be called upon to do in the future. Her parents had

always sheltered *her*, protected *her*. Shielded her as much as possible from disappointment, from hurt, from harm. She had lived most of her life in the cocoon of their love. Now it was her turn and she was afraid she wasn't up to it. *She had to be up to it. There was no other way. There was no one else.*

"*I can't go through this alone,*" her father had said. Neither can I! Coryn screamed silently.

Coryn felt the sobs coming, coming up through her tight chest, into her throat, choking her as she turned her head, gasping for air.

At the far end of the pool, she reached out with one hand, pulled herself against the side. The swimmers on both sides kept on swimming. She put her head down against the hands gripping the rail. Oh, God, I can't, I can't! *Yes you can, and you will.* She raised her head. Had someone spoken? *I will never leave you or forsake you.* Joshua 1:5. Those words from scripture learned a long time ago returned to her memory. She remembered she had received a medal in Sunday school for memorizing. She did not have to go it alone.

Strange, common thought was that it was in church you received inspiration, guidance, comfort. But isn't God everywhere? His spirit is not dependent on time or place or circumstance. He had given her this as a tool. Swimming as a coping skill. And it was working. She emerged from the pool, her body tingling from the exercise, knowing it had been worth the effort.

She pulled herself up, sat on the side of the pool, stripped off her cap, shook out her hair. She could go home now. Somehow comforted, strengthened, to face whatever there was to face.

She showered, changed into her sweatshirt, pulled on pants, sneakers, then went out into the damp morning. She drove through the quiet streets, past houses where people were just getting up, cooking breakfast, men dressing for work, children for school. She saw a boy on a bike delivering newspapers.

Then just a little ahead, on the left-hand side of the road, coming through the mist, she saw a figure, jogging. As she got closer, she could see who it was. Her hands tightened on the steering wheel. She saw his face, his intense expression. Hair dampened into waves fell on his broad forehead as he ran steadily forward. Mark. She passed him, not knowing whether he saw or recognized her. For a moment all the old feelings she had for him welled up within her. If only it could have been different...if they had met some other time...under other circumstances. It might have been different....

Chapter Nineteen

One morning after her swim, while waiting to turn in her locker key, Coryn happened to glance at the bulletin board. There, notices of various community events were posted. Her gaze caught an announcement.

CAREGIVERS HELD MONDAY
AFTERNOONS AT 3:00 P.M.
If you are or know someone who is a caregiver for a loved one, this is a group of concerned people who meet once a week to share their problems, receive help, advice, encouragement.

Coryn turned away, handed her key to the clerk behind the counter and started to leave the building. But something drew her back. Quickly she pulled out a small memo pad and pencil from her handbag, jotted down the address of the meeting.

Driving home, she wondered why she'd done that. She remembered Dr. Iverson's answer to her question, *What can I do?* "Find out all you can about your mother's disease so you'll know what to expect, how to help your father." She hadn't really done that. All she'd done was watch helplessly as her mother became slower, more forgetful and vague. What she *had* done was take care of herself. Keep herself from falling to pieces. But that wasn't enough. More was going to be required of her. She needed just what that group seemed to offer—advice, encouragement. Maybe she should check it out. Go at least once. See what it was like.

It took all Coryn's inner strength to go to that first meeting. It was admitting something she didn't want to admit. That, as a family, they were in severe crisis. To acknowledge that they were facing something so dreadful, so frightening that she had almost become paralyzed. That first time Coryn had sat there in the circle of folding chairs, her arms crossed, not entering in, not sharing, not participating.

But something had happened there. She had seen people share their pain, their raw grief, pour out their deepest feelings, some of them negative ones. No one had criticized, no one had condemned or told them they shouldn't be feeling that way. All Coryn had seen was warmth, compassion, friendliness. There had even been some laughter.

She had gone back the next Monday and the next. Then one day a middle-aged man spoke about his wife. He was a good-looking man in his middle fifties, an executive type, solid and certainly not someone you would suspect of deep emotion or sensitivity.

"Alzheimer's is called the 'long goodbye.' It's not like a stroke or a heart attack where a loved one goes suddenly, quickly. The family has to watch the person they know and love die by inches, lose them little by little. It's harder than most people realize. They desperately want to hold on to the former personality they knew, not accept this stranger that person has become." His voice cracked. "I'm losing my dearest friend, the love of my life—"

At that point something inside Coryn broke. Tears welled up in her then poured out like an erupting dam. She put her head in her hands and sobbed heartbrokenly. She felt a stir around her, then arms hugging her, hands patting her, someone handing her a box of tissues. They just let her cry. When at last she came to a stop, she felt surrounded by love and understanding, sympathy of the deepest kind.

After that, Mondays were as much a part of her healing process as the daily swims. Coryn knew she was changing, that there was a new depth of feeling for others, for suffering of all kinds. She was growing and, as in all kinds of growth, there were growing pains.

Reading became another resource. Not the bestsellers and novels that she used to enjoy. Now she searched bookstore shelves, asked some of the members in the Monday group what books they had found helpful. She regularly went to bookstores and concentrated on the self-help and religion sections. She found C. S. Lewis's and Catherine Marshall's books particularly helpful.

Still, she felt she should do something more. She had the distinct feeling that more was expected of her. What, she wasn't sure. She prayed that God would direct her path. Tell her what to do.

Every day when she drove to the pool, she passed Shady Nook Rest Home. She wasn't sure when she first began to notice the sign. However, after she did, she could not seem *not* to see it.

Coryn had a natural aversion for nursing homes. From TV she retained fleeting impressions of corridors filled with old people strapped into wheelchairs, others leaning on walkers. Wrinkled faces, with vacant expressions, bleary eyes, hollow cheeks and waddling chins. She suppressed a shudder just imagining what it must be like at Shady Nook. What it would be like to be confined there.

Day after day, an urgency grew within Coryn that she was supposed to do something. Take some kind of step. Although she recoiled from the idea, the conviction grew that it had something to do with Shady Nook Rest Home. It took root in her mind and heart. At last she could avoid it no longer.

One morning on her way back from swimming, something compelled her to swing into the Shady Nook parking lot. For a full minute, she stayed in the car, her hands clutching the steering wheel, not wanting to let go.

"I don't want to do this," she said aloud between clenched teeth.

It didn't matter. In another few seconds she was out of the car, walking up the steps and entering the lobby of the overheated building. Immediately the smells of disinfectant, cooking, plastic mingled, wrinkling Coryn's nose in distaste.

She forced herself to go up to the reception desk where a plump, gray-haired woman talked on the phone. Coryn felt the strong urge to turn and run. But she made herself stay until the woman was off the phone. She glanced at Coryn. "Yes?" she said. "Visiting hours are not until two."

"I didn't come to visit," Coryn said tightly. Then she heard herself ask, "I just wondered if you needed volunteers? Helpers of any kind."

The woman's eyebrows lifted alarmingly. She looked at Coryn skeptically, taking in her still-damp hair, her gray sweats, running shoes. "Do we need help? Volunteers? We certainly do. What do you have in mind?"

"What do you need doing?"

"Good heavens! Everything! Clerical. Setting up food trays. Feeding patients. Taking them to physical therapy. You name it, we need it," the woman declared. Then, as if in second thought, "Do you have any training?"

"No, not really. But I think I could do any of the things you just mentioned."

"Good girl!" The woman smiled broadly. "When can you start?"

It wasn't easy. It was very hard for Coryn. But she knew she was doing what she'd been directed to do.

Soon Coryn became a regular volunteer at Shady Nook Rest Home. In order to report to work the early shift, Coryn got her hair cut in a short style to minimize the drying time after her morning swim.

The overworked staff at Shady Nook Rest Home welcomed her gratefully. She soon became one of their favorites.

She was dependable, reliable. She always showed up on time, never phoned in with excuses not to report, worked diligently at whatever task assigned.

It didn't take long for Coryn to realize she was the one who was benefiting most by coming. Every time she spooned soup into a mouth twisted by a stroke, wiped dribble from a chin, assisted some disabled elderly person from bed to chair, it was as if she heard an inner encouragement, "Assuredly, I say to you, inasmuch as you did it to one of the least of these My brethren, you did it to Me."

Coryn knew she was on training ground. One day, she didn't know when, or how soon, her own beloved mother might need this kind of care. God was preparing her for whatever was to come.

One afternoon as Coryn was stacking lunch trays into their rack in the kitchen area, Mrs. Dilworth the director of the nursing home spoke to her.

"Miss Dodge, I'd like to speak to you for a few minutes, if you would stop by my office before you leave today?"

"Yes, of course," Coryn replied, wondering what she had done or not done, why and about what the director wanted to talk to her. She finished her task then went on to spray the vinyl table tops in the dining room and wipe the chrome surfaces. Funny, how she took pride in doing even the menial tasks assigned. It was also a matter of pride, doing a job well. Better watch that, she reminded herself, remembering what C. S. Lewis warned in *Mere Christianity*. Trying to be perfect at whatever you do had its traps.

Finishing up, Coryn took off her blue volunteer smock and hung it in her locker in the staff room. Then went down the hall to the director's office.

At her knock a pleasant voice invited her to come in. Coryn opened the door and entered. She had never been in here before and she was surprised to find it looked decidedly unbusinesslike. The walls were painted a warm coral, a flourishing philodendron in a basket hung in the window and on a desk was a blossoming African violet.

Mrs. Dilworth gave her a welcoming smile, "Do sit down, Miss Dodge. I've been wanting to talk to you but as you know this place keeps me extremely busy and the days go by...well, you understand."

Coryn took a seat in one of two velour upholstered chairs opposite the director's desk.

Mrs. Dilworth appeared to be in her mid-forties. She had a brisk, professional manner but twinkling eyes behind half glasses which hung from a chain around her neck. Her hair was a shade of auburn that perhaps was not its natural color but always perfectly coiffed.

"I particularly want to commend you on your performance as a volunteer. Ever since you started here I've had glowing reports from members of our staff as well as our residents."

"Thank you, that's very kind," Coryn murmured, pleased by the compliment.

"The reason I've asked you to come for this little chat today is, I wonder if you'd like to take on another kind of work here? You see, I've observed you, Miss Dodge, and your natural rapport with the ladies you come in contact with as a volunteer. You seem to be able to make them feel that you're really interested in them as individuals, make them feel special."

"Well, I've come to be very fond of them."

"Yes, that's obvious, Miss Dodge." Mrs. Dilworth beamed. "That is why I'd like to suggest that you take over our Arts and Crafts program one day a week. The person who has been doing this is moving. Her husband is being transferred and we've been looking for someone who is creative and patient, *that* is almost equally important here. Some of our residents have various disabilities that make them unable to be very dextrous, as you very well know—but they enjoy the break in their schedule that this sort of change offers and they can try making simple things." She paused. "I've seen the little cards and things you put on the trays and I've been touched as well as impressed. It is the sort of extra effort we like our residents to receive but seldom have been able to supply it." Mrs. Dilworth tilted her head inquiringly. "Do you think you may want to take this on?"

"I've never thought of doing something like this. The things you mention, well, I just did them for fun, really. And the ladies *do* seem to enjoy and appreciate them."

"Exactly. That's just the sort of thing I mean." Mrs. Dilworth nodded her head. "Easy, simple crafts that most of them will be able to handle. And just have a good time trying."

The more she thought about it the more excited Coryn became. All sorts of craft projects began forming in her mind.

The two women began exchanging various ideas Coryn could teach the ladies to make with a minimum of materials or skill.

"I see I had only to mention this and you're already way ahead of me." Mrs. Dilworth smiled. "We can get well-intentioned people, fine volunteers to help us with the practical tasks but people of creativity and artistic ability are not so readily available. It would be a great favor to us if you would agree to do this job."

It began as such a small thing but within weeks the afternoon Arts and Crafts session in the recreation room became the focal point of the week. Certainly for the residents and also for Coryn. She found she was always trying to think of new items to present to her eager participants each time. The best part of it was their enthusiasm. How the old eyes shone with anticipation when she arrived those afternoons, how even the ones whose hands were troubled with arthritis and couldn't handle a pair of scissors easily, still looked forward to the afternoon. Often the room rang with laughter, and quavery voices were raised happily as they worked and chatted.

One afternoon, Coryn was cleaning up after a hilarious session making Easter bunny baskets for centerpieces at each table in the dining room. She found Mrs. Dilworth standing at the entrance of the recreation room.

"Well, Miss Dodge, you seem to have had a successful afternoon. All the ladies seemed cheerful and lively."

"Yes, it was great fun," Coryn agreed.

Mrs. Dilworth's expression turned thoughtful, "You've really done a remarkable job in this program. I wonder, have you ever thought of it as a career? Occupational therapy? There's such a great need for it. Not only in places such as this, but in other institutions for victims recuperating from accidents and other traumas, for the physically and mentally challenged. People with that spark of creativity and the most important ingredient, compassion and understanding are rare."

"I've never even considered it. In fact, I don't think I ever considered there was a career possibility in work like this," Coryn answered.

"I suggest you should look into it. I believe the

local college has a course. Classes you could take. Why don't you check it out?"

Mrs. Dilworth planted a small seed that day. One that began to grow in Coryn the more she thought about it. What she had been desperately searching for was a purpose for her life. Now a new direction had been pointed out to her. One for which she had a natural talent. A gift as Mrs. Dilworth had put it. Scripture said, "All good gifts come from above." Was this *her* gift?

Coryn was awed how it had come, by a seemingly circuitous route. Yet she was convinced nothing happened by chance. "God works in mysterious ways." Coryn had heard that phrase most of her life. Now she believed it.

When she investigated the courses the local college offered, she found there were two classes starting in the spring semester. She signed up for both. One was a psychology class, another in communications skills, both requisites for a degree as an occupational therapist. There were other courses she would have to take to earn enough credits to actually become a qualified therapist.

Coryn added school two evenings a week. For the first time in her life felt she was doing what she was supposed to be doing, that she had found her niche.

To have a goal for herself was the best therapy she could have found, she soon realized. Instead of groping just to maintain her own emotional balance in her increasingly difficult family situation, she now had a definite purpose, a potential new career, which offered her the fulfillment and satisfaction she'd been searching for.

April

Chapter Twenty

Recently, Mark had had trouble sleeping. He'd taken to watching late-night TV or reading until his eyelids grew heavy and he dropped off midsentence, the book fallen on his chest. He'd wake up sandy-eyed and sluggish, the bedside light still burning, the morning news programs coming on.

Since he'd stopped seeing Coryn he'd lost track of the passing of days, the weeks going by. He'd buried himself in work, laboring over his columns, writing at home in his study at his desk computer. Time didn't seem to have much meaning. It was just space to fill up.

Then one morning he was awakened by Ginny's small, round face close to his, bending over him. Tugging at his pajama sleeve, she said in an insistent voice, "Wake up, Daddy."

He blinked, struggling to get his eyes fully opened.

"Mrs. Aguilar is sick so you'll have to take me."

He sat up on one elbow. "Take you where?"

"To church, of course," she explained patiently.

"Church?" he echoed blankly.

The fuzziness in his brain began to clear and he also became aware that Mrs. Aguilar, bundled into a purple chenille bathrobe, smelling suspiciously of menthol, was standing in the bedroom doorway. A startling sight since Mark had never seen the housekeeper in anything but a flowered housedress, starched apron, her salt-and-pepper hair braided around her head in a neat coronet. Her face looked puffy and flushed, her eyes glazed.

"I'm sorry, Mr. Emery, I'm afraid I've got a flu bug," she croaked. She touched her gauze-swathed throat. Obviously it was a bad case. He had never known Mrs. Aguilar to have a day's sickness.

Still, he felt vaguely annoyed at the way both were staring at him. It wasn't enough that the one day a week he had to sleep in had been disturbed, they clearly expected something else. What it was hadn't yet sunk in. He managed to be reasonably sympathetic.

"That's too bad. You go back to bed. I'll manage breakfast." He reached for his bathrobe. "Have you taken anything?"

"Two aspirins and some tea with lemon," she replied.

"Daddy," Ginny began again, "you'll have to take me..."

"To church, Mr. Emery," Mrs. Aguilar said. "Maybe you've forgotten. Today is Easter Sunday and Ginny is in the program."

"*Easter?* What program?" he growled, knowing he sounded like a disgruntled bear.

"*Daddy!*" protested Ginny. "You *know*. I told you. It's the Flowering of the Cross. The kids bring flowers and put them on the cross. Mrs. Wiley, our Sunday school teacher, says it sym—sym—" Ginny's little face screwed up with the difficulty of pronouncing the word.

"Symbolizes," Mrs. Aguilar supplied.

"Symbolizes," Ginny repeated carefully. "Symbolizes the Resurrection," she finished proudly.

Mark was sitting up now, acutely conscious that Mrs. Aguilar had not budged. She was still standing in the doorway, arms crossed. "Well, now, look, honey, Daddy isn't much for..." He stopped, ashamed of making excuses before Ginny's solemn brown eyes, Mrs. Aguilar's accusatory stare. He swallowed and began again. "What I mean is, why don't we go somewhere for breakfast, say, the Pancake House? You'd like that, wouldn't you? Then, maybe this afternoon—"

Ginny shook her head vehemently. "No, Daddy. I *have* to go to church. It's *Easter*. Besides, they're counting on me for the program. We got the flowers yesterday, yellow daisies, bluebells." Her prim little voice turned suddenly hopeful. "Couldn't we go to the Pancake House *after* church?"

From the doorway, Mrs. Aguilar said pointedly, "These things mean a great deal to a child, Mr. Emery."

Mark sighed. He'd lost. They'd won.

"Okay, I'll grab a quick shower and shave. How much time have I got?"

Ginny twirled happily out of the room, calling back over her shoulder, "Service is at eleven, but *we* have to be there by ten-thirty!"

Mark hauled himself out of bed and into the bathroom. Under the needle spray of the showerhead, he came stingingly awake. He felt guilty. He'd only half listened to Ginny's regaling him with her Sunday-school class's plans. The truth was, he'd been preoccupied with thoughts of Coryn.

Had he done right breaking it off? So abruptly? There was so much at stake in making a commitment. Finding the right person for himself was one thing. Finding the right stepmother for Ginny was something else altogether. He hadn't been sure how Coryn felt about taking on a ready-made family. And was she really over that relationship in L.A.? She hadn't talked much about that, either. No question he had been physically attracted to Coryn. She was lovely to look at, but more than that superficial beauty was intelligence, humor. There was a special quality about her, a sensitivity that was definitely appealing. He had never really asked her how she felt about children. He didn't know. And someone else's child...an adopted one? But she had seemed to love Ginny and Ginny had taken to her right away.

Had he made things too complicated? Put up too many obstacles? Ones of his own making? Afraid of risking rejection? Had he messed up royally?

He was just toweling off when a sharp knock came

at the bathroom door. "Mr. Emery, it is ten o'clock," came Mrs. Aguilar's husky voice.

"Okay. I'm almost done." He lathered his face, quickly started shaving. Next he heard Ginny's impatient, "Daddy, aren't you ready yet?"

"In a minute!" he snapped, then knowing he sounded cross, added, "Honey."

She was waiting, all dressed in a new ruffled dress, lace-trimmed white anklets, shiny black-patent Mary Janes. She looked adorable and Mark felt the familiar heart tug, wishing Shari could see her. *Maybe she can*, a strange voice seemed to say in his head.

"Here are her flowers, Mr. Emery." Mrs Aguilar handed him a fragrant small bouquet wrapped in moistened plastic wrap.

"Hurry, Daddy, I don't want to be late."

Mark exchanged an indulgent smile with Mrs. Aguilar.

"Okay, we're all set." And he held out his hand for Ginny to take.

Outside, a pale sun was pushing through the clouds in an overcast sky. North-coast weather, even on Easter, Mark thought as he put Ginny in the car. He helped her fasten her seat belt so her dress wouldn't be crushed. Then he lay the flowers carefully on the back seat, got in, started the engine and backed out of the driveway.

He walked with Ginny to the door of her Sunday-school class and left her there. She was smiling shyly and clutching her flowers. The teacher was at the door and seemed surprised to see him. He explained about the housekeeper, and Mrs. Wiley nodded sympathetically. "There's a lot of it going around. But it's nice to see *you*, Mr. Emery. I know Ginny is happy you came."

Mark felt the warmth rise into his face. He didn't need to be reminded he hadn't been to church since Shari's funeral. He couldn't explain why. It wasn't that he wasn't a believer. He *was*. He and Shari had gone to church regularly. It was just that after she was gone... Well, he didn't have to explain to anyone. God knew why. At least, the God Mark understood did.

There were clusters of people moving up the steps and into the church. Men in dark suits, women in pretty pastel dresses. After a whispered confrontation with an usher, Mark was escorted to one of the pews marked Parents. Luckily there was a seat on the aisle.

Above the altar was a magnificent stained-glass window depicting Christ as the Good Shepherd. Mark had always loved the Bible story of the one out of the ninety-nine that Jesus searched for until he found it and brought it back into the fold. Sunlight was beginning to stream in through the glass, illuminating and enhancing the colors. Mark sat in quiet contemplation of a favorite image, feeling a certain peace beginning to flow over him.

The organ began playing and white-surpliced choir members filed in and took their places, voices raised loudly, proclaiming, "This is the day that the Lord hath made, Let us rejoice and be glad in it."

There was a stirring and shuffling as the congregation stood, and with the rustling of the pages of the hymnals joined in the chorus. From the back of the church the children came down the aisle to the seats reserved for them in front. Ginny allowed herself one sidelong glance and a tiny smile of satisfaction as she passed and saw he was safely seated with the other parents.

With the close of the opening hymn, a youthful-looking minister accompanied by rosy-cheeked boys in red cassocks and starched surplices, entered from the sacristy. He mounted the pulpit and waited until, with great shifting and creaking, people settled into the wooden benches. A hushed expectancy filled the church.

In a surprisingly deep, resonant voice the minister declared, "Today we celebrate the glorious good news. 'I am the Resurrection and the Life. He that believeth in Me shall not die...'"

But Shari was dead, Mark mentally corrected. *"...but shall liveth forever in the place I have prepared for those who love Me."* The phrase seemed to echo in Mark's mind. Shari had loved Jesus with all her heart. Her whole life had been a testimony, a witness. She had touched everyone she encountered. After her death, people Mark hadn't even known had written, sent condolence cards, messages. Shari couldn't ever be *really* gone, as long as people who loved her remembered.

Mark brought his attention back to what the young minister was saying so earnestly. He found himself leaning forward intently.

"Two of the hardest things in the world are to accept death and to accept life. To accept death only requires our faith. The great tragedy is not accepting the miracle of life. The gift God has given each of us with endless possibilities. Finding beauty in all the things around us, nature, creatures, weather, the people we know, the people we are yet to meet, who will bring us new evidences of God's caring. Life has many unexplained mysteries. We must accept them all as His gifts. The light, the shadow, the pain as well as the joyous times of happiness, and laughter. He wants us to meet it all with courage, serenity and hope.''

The minister pointed to the bare cross at the foot of the altar. ''The fact of death must be accepted but not with an unforgiving grief. Love that existed in life is real and lasts beyond death. What we have shared, what we have given and received on earth will remain forever.''

Mark stirred uncomfortably. The words were hitting tender spots, wounded places. Somehow what the man was saying sounded vaguely familiar. Then he remembered he had been watching Bill Moyers's program ''World of Ideas'' on TV, and one of the guests had said, *''If you can accept death, you can affirm life.''* This minister was saying practically the same thing.

''This is the day of our Lord's resurrection. Perhaps this is a day of a new beginning. We must look into our own hearts and see that here is the joy of expectation, the hope of our faith and the love that overcomes death.''

The children, prompted by their hovering teachers, began to come forward. The older ones twined greenery around the cross made of florist's wire, then one by one the smaller children placed their flowers in the empty spaces until the outline of the symbol of death had become a bower of colorful blossoms and fragrance. Glory had replaced defeat.

The minister lifted his arms, inviting the congregation to join him in the triumphant declaration, "Let us say together, 'Christ has risen. Christ has risen, indeed.'"

Mark heard voices all around him ringing out in joyous affirmation, singing "Our God Reigns," a hymn he recalled from his own boyhood Sunday-school days. His throat was too tight to join in but he did so in his heart.

He watched as Ginny went back to her place with the other children. His heart twisted with love. Ginny deserved more than a distracted father, a man clinging to the past, not sure of the future. Things were going to change.

Love was worth the risk. He wouldn't not have had Shari even for the short time they had had together. Now he felt free to open his heart again. To Coryn? Maybe. If it wasn't too late.

Outside the church, after the service, Mark thought he caught a glimpse of Coryn and Mrs. Dodge. But the courtyard was filled with people greeting each other and wishing "Happy Easter," parents exchanging compliments on their children's performance. The parking lot was crowded as well so he couldn't have got through to speak to them anyway. Besides, what would he say? He felt awkward. Embarrassed at the way he had handled the situation with Coryn.

Had he let it go too long? Was there some way he could make amends? He should at least try.

Ginny left the group of little girls with whom she had been chatting, and ran up to Mark. "Wasn't it nice, Daddy? Didn't you like it?"

Mark felt his throat tighten. He smiled down at her. Held out his hand. "Yes, honey. It was very nice."

"Did I do good, Daddy?"

"You did wonderful!" He grinned, feeling something stinging at the back of his eyes.

"Now can we go to the Pancake House, Daddy?" she asked with a little skip.

"You bet." Mark grinned again. Now they could do a lot of things.

Chapter Twenty-One

Mark couldn't sleep. Nothing new. He was finding it harder and harder to go to sleep at a decent hour. The techno thriller he'd read to get drowsy had only served the opposite purpose, leaving him wide-awake and tense with their near-life correspondence to the daily TV news.

He got up, got a glass of water and looked over the bookcase under the bedroom window for something to read that might be boring enough to induce sleep. For some reason, he pulled out Shari's well-thumbed copy of *The Road Less Traveled* by Scott Peck. Shari had bought paperback editions of best-sellers. She'd liked to highlight, underline and make notes in the margins of books she particularly liked. She'd tried to get him to read this one. Somehow he never had.

Mark went back to bed, thumped the pillows into a bunch behind his head and settled himself in his usual methodical way.

Mark's hands gripped the edges of the book as he read page after page. This writer knew what he was talking about. It was as though he understood Mark's reluctance to follow his heart with Coryn Dodge. He was *afraid*. Afraid of being rejected, afraid of the pain that might be involved in getting to know someone, letting them know you.

Everything that makes living meaningful, rich, interesting requires putting yourself out there—being vulnerable, if you will, to whatever comes with loving. But, Peck maintained, "loving is worth the risk."

Mark lay there holding the book, stunned. It was almost as if he heard Shari's voice. She had liked to read aloud to him, paragraphs, excerpts from books she was excited about. Sometimes, caught up in his own book, he had only half listened. Tonight he listened.

He got up, and after a moment's hesitation, went to the phone and dialed the Dodges' number.

The phone rang and rang. There was no answer. Slowly Mark replaced the receiver. He realized he'd made a mistake cutting off his relationship with Coryn. Could he explain that somehow. Or was it too late? His determination strengthened. Better late than never. He'd try reaching her again tomorrow.

The phone echoed hollowly in the empty house.

Driving home through the rainy night from the airport where she had just put her parents on the plane, Coryn's thoughts were muddled.

The windshield wipers made a squeaky sound as

they swept back and forth. It had been an unusually wet spring. It had been raining for what seemed weeks. On the spur of the moment, her father had declared he had to go find some sunshine.

He had made reservations for Clare and him at the Silverado Country Club in the Napa Valley, and although invited to accompany them, Coryn had refused. She urged them to go without her. They would both feel better after a few long, lazy sun-drenched days in the valley.

The phone was ringing when she came inside the house. By the time she picked up the receiver, there was only the buzzing sound on the line that meant the party who had called had hung up.

The message machine wasn't turned on, she noticed. A clutching sensation in her stomach reminded her of recent events, of Dr. Iverson's warnings that things would grow gradually worse. Clare was always turning things off that should be left on, as well as doing the opposite. Coryn went around behind her mother, checking, righting these lapses of concentration. It was nerve-racking. Worse still was the realization that this was only the beginning of things getting worse.

An involuntary shudder shivered through her. It was happening, irrevocably. More missing pieces all the time. Coryn couldn't deny it, even though she wished she could.

She wished she had someone to confide in, someone who would understand, just by listening. She couldn't bring herself to go to one of her girlfriends. Their lives were full, happy, and they had their own problems. No one wanted to carry another's burden. Especially this kind. The kind that ended only in tragedy.

Who had called? Coryn wondered. Could it have been Mark? It had been weeks since he had come on his sad "mission of mercy." He had seemed—what? As if he wanted to explain or apologize for not calling. That had made *her* feel embarrassed. She didn't want him to feel obligated. Yet there were so many unresolved things between them. She wondered about Ginny and the new kitten.

Stop feeling sorry for yourself! Face it. Whatever had almost happened between them had been abruptly cut off. His choice. Obviously. Maybe it was better this way. She had nearly fallen in love with him. Correction. She *had* fallen in love with him. And Ginny. She had truly loved the little girl, wanted to make life more—everything for her. For a few weeks, happiness had seemed possible for the three of them. She had sensed Mark felt that, too, but... Well, she had been wrong before.

Mark sat at his desk in the newsroom of the *Rockport Times*. His In box was overflowing, his Out box just as full. His computer was booted up, but the monitor was blank. He couldn't concentrate. He flipped through his notebook. He had dozens of scribbled pages of notes taken for the story he was working on. The feature the managing editor was waiting for. It looked like Chinese. He reached for the phone, dialed the number and waited. The buzz of a busy signal came. He put down the phone, waited a few minutes, tried again. The same irritating buzz.

How could it stay busy so long? He slammed down the receiver, frowning. He keyed in a header, typed "by Mark Emery." That's as far as he got. He reached for the phone again. This time he stayed with it even though it still gave off the busy signal. Forget it. Get to work. Maybe it wasn't such a good idea, after all, to try to reach Coryn. Maybe he'd burned his bridges with her. Maybe...

But maybe there was still a chance. He picked up the phone and dialed again. This time it rang!

Good! He tapped his pencil on the desktop, waiting. Waiting. There must be someone there. It had been busy only seconds ago. Why didn't someone answer? Frustrating.

Abruptly he replaced the receiver. Turned off the computer. Stood, grabbed his jacket, shrugged into it and walked through the room humming with other reporters' activity. Someone must be at home at 183 Chestnut Hills Drive. He'd take a chance it was Coryn.

There was something wrong with Ranger. For a few days he had hardly stirred from his pillowed basket in the utility room.

The morning after her parents left for Napa Valley, Coryn opened the door from the kitchen and looked in. Ranger lifted his head, his tail wagged feebly. At once she was kneeling on the floor beside him, stroking his head. "What's the matter, old fella?"

At the sound of her voice, he raised clouded eyes

adoringly. She touched him gently and he struggled to move, but could not. Coryn let her hand smooth down over his body, his hind legs, to see if he was in pain anywhere. He did not seem to be. He simply could not get up.

Worried, Coryn refilled his water dish then brought it back and placed it within easy reach. But he did not make any effort to drink. Should she call the vet? Or try to take him to the animal clinic? Hands shaking she looked up the number in the phone book and called.

When she explained her concern and described Ranger's condition, the vet's secretary said, "Well, our records show he *is* fifteen, Miss Dodge. That's quite an age for a dog."

Coryn felt instant resentment. What was that supposed to mean? The dog was *sick,* not *dying*…then she felt herself tremble, or *was* he?

"If you want to bring him in…" The crisp voice on the other end of the line sounded dubious, "We can schedule him in at three-thirty this afternoon."

Eight hours from now! Anything could happen before then. She hung up numbly and went back to Ranger. She sat down beside him, feeling helpless, infinitely sad. Ranger gave a long shuddering sigh that quivered the length of his body. Automatically she scratched behind his ears, smoothed his fur. After a while he shut his eyes and seemed to sleep. Coryn got up, tiptoed into the kitchen. She poured herself coffee, tried to swallow it over the hard lump in her throat.

She stood looking out the kitchen window. Ranger

had been a large part of her life ever since the day her father had brought the silky black, wiggly Lab puppy home for her. They had run, romped together, he wheeling, jumping and barking when she used the swings in the backyard or threw balls into the basket over the garage door. He was always waiting for her at the gate when she got home from school. Her mother said when Ranger heard the school bus, his ears jerked up and he went to the door barking to be let out to run to meet her.

When she came home from college for vacations, he seemed ecstatic with happiness. He was always eager to go with her, walking or in the car...until this time. Coryn felt guilty that when she was in L.A. she had hardly thought about him. She had been too preoccupied with Jason....

She turned and went back where Ranger lay. His breath was coming in slow trembling sighs. He's going, Coryn thought. He's going to die. Oh, Ranger. She stifled a sob.

She heard the sound of wheels on the gravel driveway and hurried to the window in time to see the Sanders Landscape Service truck pull to a stop in front. Her parents employed Joe Sanders to take care of the lawn, to keep the hedges trimmed and the flower beds weeded. Her father didn't have time anymore. She saw Joe get out, pull his tools from the back of the truck.

It was comforting somehow to see Joe, the solid, steady strength of him out there while she kept her vigil inside. It wasn't long. When she went back to sit beside Ranger again, he had stopped breathing.

He had died quietly. Coryn let the tears pour down her cheeks.

She covered him with an old soft blanket then went outside to where Joe was pruning the branches of the pyracantha bushes.

Her voice shook as she told him what had happened. "I'm going to bury him up on the hillside behind the house," she said. "But I'll need your help to lift him and get him up there."

"Sure, Miss Dodge, be glad to. We can put him in the wheelbarrow, that'll make it easier." He put down his clippers and went to his truck. He wheeled close to the back door then followed Coryn inside. Together, they carried Ranger's body, wrapped in the blanket, outside and placed it carefully in the wheelbarrow.

"Would you want me to bury him for you, Miss Dodge?"

Fighting tears, Coryn shook her head. "No, thanks, Joe, he was my dog. I want to say goodbye to him by myself."

"Yep. I understand. That dog was sure enough *your* dog." Joe nodded. "But I can wheel him up there, can't I? It's pretty heavy."

"Thanks, Joe, that would be fine." Silently they made the journey. Coryn carrying the shovel Joe had handed her, he pushing the wheelbarrow.

He lifted the dog out of the barrow and placed him on the grass. He took off his duck-billed cap for a moment before replacing it then walked back down the hill.

Coryn began to dig. The earth was moist from the

recent rains, but it was still hard work. She was breathing hard, and perspiration beaded her forehead and upper lip. Ranger was a big dog. She wanted his grave to be long and deep enough for him. She dug hard. Her heart was pounding, she was panting with the exertion. She wasn't sure how long she had been digging, when she heard movement behind her, her name spoken. "Coryn."

Her shovel midair, she spun around and saw Mark coming up on the crest of the hill. She let the shovel drop, leaned on the handle, slowing her deep breaths. Finally, she gasped, "Mark!" Then, "What are *you* doing here?"

"I've been trying to get you. Tried to call last night, but there was no answer. Then this morning, I called several times and the line was busy. I thought I'd just take a chance, come by this morning and see you."

Coryn stared at him, bewildered. Why had he been calling her? Trying to reach her? It didn't make sense. She glanced at Ranger's blanket-covered body then back at Mark.

He nodded. "Joe Sanders told me what happened. I'm sorry." He paused. "Really sorry."

At the sincere sympathy in his voice, tears rushed into her eyes again. She couldn't stop them, and a harsh sob thrust from her throat.

In a minute, he was beside her, arms around her, holding her close, his chin on her head. She leaned against him, sobbing. "I know, I know," she heard him whisper soothingly.

In a world of terrorist bombs, civil wars and upheaval all over the globe, to some it might have seemed almost shameful to cry over the death of an old dog. Mark had lost his wife! What must he think of this grief? But as he continued to hold her, gently stroking her hair, her cheek resting against his shoulder, Coryn had a revelation. Mark *knew* how she felt. By his knowing, he made it not seem foolish to grieve so for a dog. In fact, his empathy made it seem right to mourn for a dog you have loved.

After a while, her sobs had turned to long, drawn-out gasps. He handed her a clean handkerchief to wipe her eyes and blow her nose. Sniffling, she said, "I didn't mean to dump on you like that."

"Not at all. I'm glad I was here. I understand."

Coryn looked up at him and knew he did.

"Let me help," he said quietly. He took off his tan corduroy sport coat and laid it on the ground. Then he picked up the shovel she had let drop, and began lifting large shovelfuls of dirt.

She leaned back against a nearby tree, watching him work in a smooth, even swinging movement.

At last the hole was dug, long and wide enough to gently lift Ranger and place him on a pile of leaves Coryn had gathered to cushion him in the ground. They both stood looking down at him for a minute then Coryn felt Mark take her hand in his, press it. She felt he was joining her in a silent prayer. Her heart was so full she could not voice the words. But it was a prayer of thanksgiving to God for having had Ranger as long as she had. From the time he had been a shiny, black puppy, through all the years of loving companionship. A prayer for allowing her the privilege of seeing him out of life with dignity and affection.

After that quiet moment, slowly they took turns shoveling the dirt over him, packing it down. They both searched for stones to circle the spot where he lay.

"I think Dad will want to have some kind of marker made for him," Coryn said. "Thank you for coming, Mark. Your being here just now—well, it meant a great deal."

"I'm glad I was here," he said. "I want to be here for you, Coryn. That is, if you'll let me."

Coryn felt too worn-out, her heart too bruised to take in all that might mean. Maybe later, when she had had time to heal a little, she would remember and think about what was unspoken between them. Now it was enough to appreciate his sensitivity and compassion for what she was feeling.

Mark replaced the shovel in the wheelbarrow and together they walked back down the hill.

Chapter Twenty-Two

The rain splashed noisily on the flagstone patio, played a staccato drum on the windows. Coryn was curled on the living-room sofa, reading. Earlier, her father had called from Silverado Country Club saying they were going to stay a few days longer.

"Your mother's really enjoying being here, looking tanned and rested. I think it's done her a world of good."

Coryn found herself puzzled by her father's confidence. Was her mother really doing that well? She had her good days and bad days and maybe that's what he was reporting. Today. It was just as well. To live each day as it came, praying for strength to get through whatever lay ahead. That's what she was trying to do.

Since Dr. Iverson had confirmed her mother's diagnosis, Coryn had read everything she could find about Alzheimer's. The Caregivers group had been immensely helpful. She had tried to persuade her father to come to one of the meetings. So far he hadn't. Was he still in denial in a way? What she had learned was that Alzheimer's disease was a treacherous one that affected the entire family. The unknown was the frightening part. It was, she thought, like those antique maps of the world where at the edge of the known world was printed the warning, *"Beyond this point lie sea dragons."* Coryn felt the more she learned the better she could anticipate these "dragons" and help her mother.

She had also bought inspirational tapes to listen to on her tape player earphones while out on her long walks. She knew she had to be strong and resourceful. It was necessary for at least one person in a family who had a member suffering from this illness to be as knowledgeable as possible.

Coryn had had to accept the harsh fact that as each day slipped by, more and more of her mother's world became blurred. Little by little the person Coryn had loved was becoming a stranger.

This acceptance had not come easily. It had come with anguish, weeping bitter tears long into many nights. In spite of her own pain, Coryn knew she had to be strong. She couldn't fall apart. Her father leaned on her. Most of all, she wanted to be able to see her mother safely home.

After she hung up from her father's call, she went back to the book she was reading. It was one she had found quite by chance. Or had it been? Coryn was beginning to find out that nothing in life was solely by chance. In this case, it had turned out to be exactly what she needed.

While browsing in a bookstore, she had discovered C. S. Lewis books. In his works she had found a treasure trove of help. She had seen the movie *Shadowland* and been much moved by Lewis's love story with Joy Davidson. She hadn't realized he had written so many books, most of them spiritual. The title *A Grief Observed* seemed to leap out at her from among the others.

Although the content was profound, the writing style had such clarity it spoke to the very heart. Now she went back to what she was reading when the phone had rung.

In the poignant, poetic words the author warned that to love anything—even an animal—means risking heartbreak and pain. But the alternative, not to love at all, sealing your heart away in a coffin of selfishness, would change a feeling heart into something unbreakable, impenetrable. Even inhuman.

Coryn drew in her breath, put her finger in between the pages to mark her place, closed the book for a moment, letting the truth of those words sink in. That is exactly what she had been doing. Afraid of being hurt, she had withdrawn, closed herself off. Not even let herself feel the exquisite pain of Ranger's death fully. She had not allowed herself to love Ginny. She had never taken her the dollhouse family. What did it matter if Mark didn't feel romantically toward her, she still could be a friend to his little girl. And even to Mark. Certainly he had shown himself to be *her* friend and a friend to her family, when he had come to tell them the rumors about Clare, offer help.

He had surely been a friend the day she buried Ranger. Even before that…maybe. He said he'd been trying to get in touch with her, she had pulled back. Why? Wouldn't being friends with a person of Mark's caliber be a good thing? There were other kinds of love. Valuable kinds, enriching kinds. C. S. Lewis and Joy Davidson had started out being friends. Anything was possible if you allowed yourself to be open to it.

Just then the front doorbell sounded above the thundering downpour. She glanced at the mantel clock. It was after nine. Who could be coming by this late in the evening?

She turned on the porch light and looked through the peephole. She saw a man's figure, shoulders hunched against the wind and rain. She thought she recognized him. She unlocked and opened the door. A gust of rain-driven wind tugged at it, and she had to grip it with her other hand to keep it from blowing back upon her. It *was* Mark.

She became suddenly conscious of how she looked. She had on one of her dad's old flannel shirts, stirrup pants, fuzzy bedroom slippers. But she couldn't let Mark stand outside in the pouring rain.

"Coryn, I hope I'm not disturbing, interrupting anything?"

"No. Come in before you get soaked."

"Sure it's not a bad time? I came—on the spur of the moment. I was working late, or trying to, and was on my way home when—I think we need to talk… Is that okay?"

"Of course, come in." She ran her fingers through her hair self-consciously.

He stepped into the foyer, his raincoat was dripping. "I know I should have called but—actually, I drove around the block several times before stopping." He halted.

She was thinner than he remembered, looked as though she'd lost weight. Her eyes seemed larger than ever and her mouth, the mouth he had loved kissing, looked more vulnerable.

"Why don't you take off your coat, it's soaked." Coryn tried to sound normal. She felt tense, wondering what Mark had come to talk to her about. Whatever it was, it must be important. "Come into the living room, I've got a fire going."

He shrugged off his coat, handed it to her. She hung it up then he followed her into the living room.

"Are your parents here?" he asked.

"No, they're still away." She gestured to the armchair on the other side of the fireplace and Mark sat down.

"How are things going? I mean, how is your mother?"

"At the moment, at least, Dad says she's doing fine. They're at the Silverado Country Club. Long, lazy days in the sun. He's playing a few rounds of golf. She's resting on the terrace." Coryn paused. "There nothing's demanded of her. She doesn't have to perform even ordinary household tasks. So I think Dad feels she's improving." She sighed. "Of course, we know that's impossible."

"That's tough. I know you're going through some really hard times."

"I guess no one escapes. Everyone has something in their lives..." She paused, thinking of Mark's losing his wife just when everything seemed to be going so well for them.

"Yes, but when you're going through it, you can't help but ask why? Why me? Why us? But then you realize *why not me?*"

They were silent for a few moments, then Mark said, "You must be curious as to why I came by tonight. I hardly know where exactly to begin, but I think I owe you an apology."

Coryn held up one hand to halt him, shaking her head. "No, Mark, of course not—"

"But I think I do, Coryn. At least an explanation. I've been wrong about a lot of things and I'm afraid I hurt you. The last thing I ever wanted to do was that. Because, the truth is, I..." He stopped as if not knowing how to go on.

Coryn held her breath. Waiting. The only sound in the room was the slow ticking of the mantel clock, the hiss of the fire as a log broke apart. Her heart, however, had begun to beat loudly.

"The truth is, Coryn, I foolishly wrote you out of my life. Because I was afraid. Afraid it might not be real, but more than that, that it might be too painful. I wasn't willing to risk getting involved with anyone again. I felt I had all I could handle just bringing up Ginny, holding down my job. A relationship takes time to grow, and I wasn't willing to take a chance. It seemed too risky somehow."

"Mark, you don't have to tell me this. I think I understand. Right now my life is very complicated. My parents need me in a way they've never needed me before. I've a lot of growing to do myself to try to meet that need." She paused. "A relationship can be absorbing and demanding and—"

"Yes, but that's where I was wrong, Coryn. Life doesn't get any smoother, any simpler. We both have difficulties, that's true. But this thing between us— the attraction I believe we both feel—if it is real, and I think it is, testing it will prove it. Sharing some of the burdens, as the saying goes, makes them lighter. And there are joys along the way, too. I don't regret having known the happy times with Shari. Not to have known her would have been far worse. A loss of another sort. Do you see what I mean?"

He reached over and took Coryn's hand, looked deeply into her eyes as if hoping to find what he was looking for there.

"Ginny misses you, Coryn. She's asked me several times when the three of us are going to do something together. Don't you think it would be worth it if we started spending time together again?"

Coryn gently pulled her hand away, stood up and moved over to the window. Rain pelted the windowpanes. She put her hands against the coolness of the glass then on her cheeks. They were flaming hot.

"Coryn." He spoke her name like a caress.

She felt shaky, her heart thrummed. Slowly she turned around from the window, faced him.

Mark rose, stood looking at her, waiting for her answer. Coryn's face was pale, there were smudges under her eyes as though she had not been sleeping much. But even without makeup, even in that shapeless baggy top, to him, she had never looked so appealing, so desirable. He said her name again, this time like a question. "Coryn?"

She didn't remember taking a step toward him or him coming to her. She only knew that when Mark held out his arms she went into them and he was kissing her. There was a sweet tenderness in that kiss, as if time had lost all meaning.

When the kiss ended, Mark held her tight, then before loosening his hold, kissed her again. Slowly they drew apart. A marvelous feeling of warmth, gladness swept over her. She stepped back.

They gazed at each other with a new awareness, a kind of recognition of what had just happened. Mark's smile was wide, hopeful. Coryn's was wobbly.

"So, shall we give it another try?" he asked.

Her breath quickened. "Yes, let's," she whispered.

Later, sitting side by side on the sofa in front of the flickering fire, Mark's arm around her, they said all the things their hearts had longed to say to each other. They talked of the past, of Shari, of Ginny, of what they would do next and of the future.

"What it all comes down to is letting go, doesn't it?" Mark asked. "Letting go of old memories, old expectations, lovingly, without regret or bitterness. Remembering the happy times, hoping there will be others.

"No one has any guarantee of happiness, not for

anyone. No matter what they try to gain or what they try to avoid. It's part of being human. None of us knows what lies ahead. Your parents didn't. Shari and I certainly didn't. But that didn't stop us from adopting Ginny and planning for a future with her.''

Coryn thought of all the time she had wasted looking back. Agonizing over the mistakes she had made with Jason. It all seemed a long time ago now, as if it had happened to somebody else.

She looked at Mark, and was caught up in the directness and honesty of his regard. He wasn't offering her protection, shelter from whatever storms there might be in this journey they would travel together. The journey to deeper understanding, of genuine friendship, of caring. He was asking her to risk loving him and Ginny.

Whatever "dragons" lay ahead, whatever was before her, with God's help and Mark beside her, she was ready to begin.

One Year Later

Epilogue

The couple and the child scrambled over the dunes onto a beach swept clean by the morning tide. A small golden retriever puppy, all paws and wagging tail, tumbled ahead of them, barking and sliding in the deeper sand.

The child, a little girl of about seven, turned, grinned widely, displaying two missing front teeth, laughed, shouted back to the man and woman following her, "Look, Goldie loves it!"

Coryn met Mark's eyes, and the glance between them was one of mutual awareness, amusement and affection.

They caught hands and swung them as they all walked down the beach. The waves rushed to shore in foamy curves. Above them, seagulls whirled, screeching, the sound mingling with Ginny's happy cries to the rambunctious puppy.

Was it really possible to be this happy? Coryn asked herself.

The last five months had been the happiest of Coryn's life. They had been married in a small, private ceremony at the church they now attended. Coryn had wanted the wedding to take place before her mother had slipped too far from reality. Clare had looked beautiful in a blue lace gown, a wide-brimmed hat framing her still lovely face.

Coryn wanted Ginny to be part of the ceremony so she was the only attendant. Looking adorable in a smocked and ruffled dress and carrying a small bouquet of violets, she stood proud and happy at the altar with them, as they spoke their vows. It had been an unforgettable occasion.

Her mother's slow progress to oblivion was still taking its measured toll. Yet through it all, Coryn had found Mark and a love she had at one time thought out of her reach. Truly, God had been good. In every trial there was a triumph, in every loss gain.

Mark had taught her that grieving *is* the healing. To grieve the loss of a loved one is the path to healing. The length of time it takes is different for everyone. There is no set number of weeks, months, even years. It cannot be hastened. If the grieving is not suppressed, it does the healing. To be open to the grief and allow it to do its work is what is important. Help comes in all forms, understanding supportive friends, spiritual sources.

It had taken Mark more than three years to heal from Shari's death, to be ready, not to replace her, but to find another relationship was possible, to welcome the healing, to risk loving again.

Although her mother's death would not be the sudden death Shari's accident had been, but gradual, still Coryn had to learn to let her go, to allow the grieving to do its work.

Mark understood this and was there for Coryn as she slowly, painfully learned it, too. The puppy he had given her to mark their engagement, had been part of Mark's therapy to help her. Sensitively he had chosen a female *golden* retriever, not a black male one that might suppose she was meant to replace Ranger. Not to be afraid to love a dog again was another healing step for Coryn.

In the past months, Ginny had been an important part of that progress. There had been a touching bond between the little girl and Coryn's mother. They had spent time together in the sunny solarium of the Dodges' home where they had set up Ginny's dollhouse, now furnished and with its complete doll family. With some of Clare's favorite music playing in the background, Ginny had played happily in the quiet, dreamy presence of the older woman. Ginny had proven the center of a widening circle of love that included her and Mark.

After Coryn, Mark, and Ginny became a family certain changes were made. Mrs. Aguilar who had heartily approved of the marriage, offered to serve as caregiver of her mother the days Coryn went to the University pursuing her degree in occupational therapy. In the evenings, Neil Dodge took over, seeming to cherish the time spent with his beloved wife. He had mellowed in his acceptance of her illness and his devotion was unflagging. Their loving relationship was an inspiration to Mark and Coryn as they began their own life's journey together.

None of this was easy. But together they had traveled this difficult path, making the journey together. Together they had learned that "weeping may endure for the night but joy cometh in the morning."

Just then, sunshine broke through the clouds, tinting the bluffs behind them with gilded light. The wind off the ocean was crisp and smelled of brine. The surf swooped in with a roar, casting huge clumps of seaweed onto the sand. Down on the beach Ginny ran ahead, Goldie scampered along beside her.

Coryn looked over at Mark. He was looking at her. They stopped, threw their arms around each other and kissed. There was a taste of salt on his lips, but the kiss was sweet, long and infinitely tender.

Yes! It *was* possible to be this happy. Even walking in the shadow of death. In spite of everything! It would be wrong not to be happy on this beautiful day, not to appreciate it and the love that had been given her as a gift.

Coryn heard Goldie's bark, Ginny's happy laugh behind Mark's voice saying, "I love you."

* * * * *

Dear Reader,

Ever since it dawned on me at about the age of ten or eleven that all those books in the library I loved to read were written by real people, I wanted to become a writer. Telling stories seemed a wonderful way to spend my life. I am living my dream.

My goal is to write novels with unforgettable characters whose stories will linger in readers' minds long after they finish the book. Novels about challenges, choices in life and the experiences that strengthen and inspire.

I feel very privileged to be published by Steeple Hill and hope my novels will reach readers and touch them in ways that will be both entertaining and reaffirming.

With best wishes,

Jane Peart